"Irresistible?" Cam took a step closer.

Rose pushed at his chest, but laughed. "Impossible. You're impossible."

He grabbed her hand and held it, stroking her wrist with his thumb. He could feel the frantic flutter of her pulse and threaded his fingers through hers. It was all he could do to keep from pulling her closer to him.

Could they get involved? That thought scared him as much as it tempted him. Pursuing Rose meant settling down for the long haul. An image of the boxes stacked in the corner of her apartment came to mind, making him think about her and Greg moving into his house someday, making it a home.

Did he want that?

Searching her eyes, part of him wanted it very much. "I care about your son, Rose. He's a good kid and I'd never steer him wrong. I hope you know that."

She gave his hand a friendly squeeze. Her eyes had never left his, as if weighing his words. His motives. Him.

Finally, she smiled and pulled her hand away. "I believe you."

Jenna Mindel lives in northwest Michigan with her husband and their three dogs. A 2006 Romance Writers of America RITA® Award finalist, Jenna has answered her heart's call to write inspirational romances set near the Great Lakes.

An Unexpected Family

Jenna Mindel

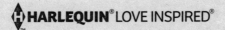

HARLEQUIN® LOVE INSPIRED®

Recycling programs
for this product may
not exist in your area.

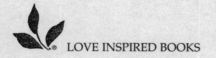

® LOVE INSPIRED BOOKS

ISBN-13: 978-1-335-42809-7

An Unexpected Family

Copyright © 2018 by Jenna Mindel

Trust in the Lord with all thine heart;
and lean not unto thine own understanding.
In all thy ways acknowledge him,
and he shall direct thy paths.
—*Proverbs* 3:5–6

A huge thank you to Ron Varga
at Varga & Varga PC for answering my many
questions about wills! Hopefully, I got it right.

For the sake of the story, I took fictional license
with the world of professional bass fishing.
Any inconsistencies are purely my own.

Chapter One

"Hey, sleepyhead." Rose Dean ruffled her eleven-year-old son's brown hair. Soon to turn twelve, the kid was growing like a weed.

Greg jerked away. "Awww, Mom, cut it out."

She watched him pad his way to the industrial fridge of the diner she'd inherited in Maple Springs, Michigan. Greg was tall like his father and she hoped the resemblance to her ex-husband remained outward. Refilling her coffee mug with freshly made brew, she said, "I like your hair."

"It's longer than yours." He finger combed his bangs away from steely gray eyes as if erasing her motherly touch.

"That's true." Her son had never liked her short hair. But for Rose, it made things easier.

Three weeks ago, a few days before Memorial Day, they'd moved up north away from her steady job as an events manager at a conference center.

Away from the steady influence of her parents, into a small town with a small high school that hopefully held smaller chances for trouble.

Rose wanted to be on her own. As much as she loved her parents and was grateful for everything they'd done for her, she didn't ever want to move back in with them. She wanted her own home. Her own life. Independence.

She could model that independence only so much for her son. Greg needed strong male role models—maybe now more than ever, living away from his grandpa—but Rose wanted a good man. A man of his word. Maybe in this pristine lakeside town there might be a good teacher or coach who Greg could look up to. Staring out the window at some of the flashy cars parked along Main Street, Rose had her doubts, but she still prayed that God would deliver.

She straightened the stack of morning receipts and stuffed them into the bottom drawer of the cash register along with her fears. She needed to trust God on this one. Easier said than done. Coming here, Rose had taken a leap of faith. She believed that the Lord had given her this opportunity, so she needed to believe He'd take care of the rest.

Hearing grumbles, she looked at Chuck and muttered under her breath, "Now what?"

A grumpy cook had come along with her inheritance of Dean's Hometown Grille from her mother-in-law, Linda Dean. Evidently, the terms of the will had been very specific. Rose did not just inherit the building; Linda had stipulated that Rose run the diner herself until such time Greg could take over. Rose had had no idea the woman intended to leave her anything. Why would she? Linda's eldest son had abandoned Rose and Greg years before he died.

Chuck cursed and threw the spatula across the stainless-steel grill.

Rose glanced at the few remaining breakfast patrons seated near the sunny window overlooking Main. They didn't appear to hear anything. Chuck's colorful language had become more commonplace since Rose took over, and she didn't like it. Not one bit. Chuck hadn't liked her directives to rein in his tongue, either. Firing the cranky cook without a replacement wasn't an option. She couldn't cook.

Rose sighed. "What happened?"

"Burned my thumb," the cook growled.

She glanced at Greg. Her son rolled his eyes and drained his glass of milk. Chuck was no role model. He wasn't the kind of man she wanted Greg around. Rose had recently signed her son up for a summer program during the week. Although this little café was his legacy and more than likely the only reason Rose had inherited it, she couldn't fill all her son's summer vacation days with busing tables.

He was too old for day care, and Rose couldn't make Greg stay indoors upstairs until the restaurant closed at two in the afternoon. Nor did she want her son roaming around Maple Springs on his own. Not yet anyway, not until she knew more about their new hometown. Even tiny resort towns held dangers for unsupervised eleven-year-olds soon to be twelve.

The bell over the front door rang, announcing more customers. This morning had been busy. Since she had taken over the diner, they'd been busy nearly every day. Except for Sunday. Rose had started something new by closing the diner on Sundays. That had earned more complaints from the cook. *Linda never closed the diner.*

Well, Rose wasn't Linda. Despite carrying the last name, Rose wasn't a Dean. She hardly knew the family she'd married into twelve years ago, but then she'd ended up divorced five years later.

A man and woman walked inside and their laughter snagged her attention. The two greeted people they knew. The man was handsome, broad shouldered and tall with disheveled blond hair, but his bright blue eyes captured her interest. They shone like gemstones from all the way across the small dining area.

Those brilliantly colored eyes locked onto hers,

and he smiled, showing off near-perfect teeth. It wasn't a pleasant, hello-how-are-you kind of smile, either. He reacted with a lazy, I-can-show-you-a-good-time smile. This man recognized a lonely woman as if he could see straight through to her heart and the secrets locked there.

Rose ignored the hiccup of her pulse rate and looked away. What a jerk! Making eyes at her while he was with another. She nearly tore her order pad apart flipping over to a clean sheet.

Grabbing a couple menus, Rose approached their table. The woman was equally fine with long, straight blond hair and perfectly manicured nails. *Figures*.

"Are you the new owner?" The woman looked up and smiled. Her blue eyes were the same brilliant shade as the man's. Now, what were the chances of that?

Rose smiled. "I am. In fact, this is my second Saturday."

The woman held out her hand. "My name's Monica. Welcome."

"Thank you, Monica. I'm Rose Dean." She shook the woman's hand, liking her instantly even though she felt sorry for her bad taste in men. Rose had been there, done that.

Monica dug in her purse. "I'm so sorry for your loss. Everyone loved Linda and she'll be sorely missed. If I may, here's my card. Linda never wanted a website, but as a new owner, if you'd like to consider an online presence, let me know."

"Oh." Rose took the card and pocketed it. She wasn't sure she could afford to hire anyone for a website. She hadn't had a chance to go over the financials with more than a cursory glance. She didn't know what to look for and that meant hiring an accountant to find out. Another expense she wasn't yet sure she could afford.

"Nice sales pitch," the man drawled.

"Just trying to help." Monica forced another smile. "*This* is my brother, Cam Zelinsky."

"Oh." Maybe he wasn't quite as despicable as she'd first thought, but Rose knew his type and didn't take his offered hand. She gave him the menu instead. "Nice to meet you both. Our lunch special is a grilled Reuben with fries, and we serve breakfast till we close at two. Can I get either of you something to drink before ordering?"

Cam narrowed beautiful eyes. "An iced tea, no lemon."

"Just water for me, with lemon," Monica said.

Rose nodded. "Be right back."

While she was filling their drink orders, more people came in. The bell rang again, announcing a few more. Rose checked her watch. Eleven o'clock seemed awfully early for the lunch crowd, but then, this was mid-June. Summer was in full swing and many folks vacationed up north.

Although she'd never lived here before, she knew northern Michigan was a destination for vacationers and summer residents alike. Her ex-husband had once explained that nearly three-quarters of this town's residents lived here primarily in summer. In winter, Maple Springs rolled up and died.

Rose looked forward to that slowdown. But for now, she loaded her tray with more ice waters and got to work greeting customers and taking orders.

Cam took another bite of his grilled Reuben. He'd tasted better. He'd *made* better. Chuck was slipping, but then, without Linda Dean to keep him in line—

"Write so I can read it!"

Cam jerked his head toward the new owner, curious to see how she handled the cook's rudeness. *Rose.* What an apt name for a woman with such a fresh face. Her skin flushed pink, looking as soft as a petal from the flower bearing her name.

He cringed. He'd never compared a woman to a flower before.

"I don't recall seeing her at Linda's funeral." Monica watched her, too.

Dean's Hometown Grille was a small place. It had been closed for only a couple of weeks after Linda's untimely death. A restaurant couldn't afford to close their doors for long and hope to survive. Poor Rose. After giving the cook a stern look, she darted from table to table, taking orders, putting them in, picking them up. She looked overwhelmed. A gangly young kid cleared the empty tables and wiped them down.

Cam sipped his iced tea. "I remember two of the Dean boys from high school, but not the oldest. I don't remember them having a sister."

Monica shrugged. "Maybe she's a cousin or something. Word on the street is that Linda's *boys* aren't happy."

"With what?" Cam asked.

"Her getting this." His sister made a sweeping gesture.

"The *street*? Really, Monica?" Cam chuckled. Maple Springs was far from city life. The only thing remotely urbane was the people that flooded the area for a few months in summer and the winter ski season. And the trendier restaurants that came and went hoping to capture high-end patronage. Maple Springs needed this hole-in-the-wall, fifties-styled diner for the locals. It had been here for as long as Cam could remember.

The clattering sound of a plate hitting the floor followed by language he didn't often hear in public brought Cam's head up fast.

"Chuck, that's enough!" Rose hissed.

The customers fell silent as the cook stripped off his white apron and threw it at Rose. "Fine."

"Where, where are you going?" Her voice wavered.

"I've had enough of you and your scribbles. Get someone else!" With that, the cook stormed out the back with a slam of the screen door.

Rose's face flamed. She turned to the boy who had hurried to her side ready to do battle and whispered something in his ear. The kid nodded, grabbed a pitcher of water and made the rounds.

Conversation picked up slowly. A table of four that had waited too long for their orders to be taken got up and walked out while Rose cleaned up the shattered plate.

"Ow!" He felt a sharp pinch to his forearm. "What?"

Monica poked him again. "Go help her."

Cam rose to his feet with a sinking feeling. This was what becoming a better person meant. Helping someone in need. Trouble was that Rose Dean looked like a woman with a deep well of need and Cam was a shallow pan.

Her back was turned while she washed and then dried her hands. She moved to the grill and stared at it, lost.

"Do you have another apron?"

She turned to him, her eyes big and shiny. This

close, he could see they were grass green. Her hair was clipped too short for his taste and its drowsy color lay somewhere between blond and brown. "What?"

"An apron? I know how to cook." He knew what needed done and he had some time to kill. Not much, only a few days before heading for the first of three qualifying bass fishing tournaments.

The bell jingled.

She glanced at the door as more people flooded inside. The lunch crowd rolled in with a vengeance. "Uhh—"

"Hey, kid, apron?" Cam went to the sink and washed his hands.

The boy disappeared in back for a second and returned with a fresh one, but scowled as he handed it over.

"What's your name?" Cam asked as he pulled the strings around his waist and tied a bow in front.

"My son, Greg." Rose stared as if either he'd lost his mind or she had. Probably a little of both.

"Those people want to order." Cam nodded toward the dining area.

Rose scurried off.

Greg stared him down as if weighing in on Cam's motives.

Truly, he didn't have any, other than a recent

promise he'd made to God. "It's okay, kid. I've done this before. Go help your mom."

Greg not only looked satisfied with that answer, he smiled and then hurried to bus a table while Rose took another order. Cam spotted Monica sliding a few bills into the pocket of Rose's ruffled red-checkered apron before waving goodbye as she left.

"Let's see here." Cam looked over Rose's order slips and grimaced. This was going to take a minute to figure out.

euR w/ y's.

ʎo /w qɔ

Chuck had been right. Her scribbles resembled the periodic table hanging on the wall in his high school science class. Fortunately, he'd muddled through math and science. He'd worked in enough restaurants to figure out scribbled order tickets, too, even though it took time. Time he didn't have.

He glanced at Rose, remembering the specials she'd told him earlier and the letters finally made sense. A Reuben with fries and a cheeseburger with onion rings. Relief washed through him but it wasn't sweet.

He had to get back on the bass pro circuit. If he didn't qualify for next year's schedule, he'd be a goner. Without fishing, this was the best he could ever do and even that was tough when it came to reading order tickets.

He looked around, found the prep fridge and got to work making that hot grill sizzle.

It was nearly closing time and Rose made change for their last customer and laughed at something the old guy said. She had a great laugh—deep and rich sounding. Nothing fake or put on.

The front door opened with a jingle. Two men entered and Cam's stomach turned when he recognized them as Karl and Kory Dean. They raked him over with arrogant smirks reminiscent of high school days. They'd always looked down at him and called him stupid—

"Well, if it isn't Cam Zelinsky. Aren't you supposed to be fishing somewhere?" Kory didn't bother hiding a sneer.

Cam's professional fishing career was no secret, especially in Maple Springs. He'd been a guest on local outdoors shows and a few articles had been written about him in the local paper. It had been a few years since he'd won big, but no matter how well he'd done, there were always guys like the Deans who thought he was a waste of skin, wasting time chasing fish.

Wiping his hands on the front of his apron, Cam came out from behind the service counter. "Just taking a break."

"You work here?" Karl's eyebrows rose.

"Filling in." He wasn't about to let on that Chuck had defected. That guy might cool down and come back.

"Hmm." Karl looked around, as if he couldn't care less what Cam did. "Is Rose here?"

Cam scanned the diner. Rose walked the customer she'd made change for to the door and then flipped the Open sign over to show Closed. Hadn't these guys ever met her before? She was family, wasn't she? "She's right there."

Kory sized her up, looking satisfied. "Rose Dean?"

Rose turned and smiled. "Yes?"

"I'm Kory and this is Karl. We're Linda's sons."

Rose hesitated before finally reaching out her hand to each of them. "Hello."

Kory turned to him. "Will you excuse us?"

Cam glanced at Rose. If she wanted him to stay, he would. In fact he hoped she did. He didn't trust these guys, especially after what Monica had said about their not being happy with Rose inheriting the Grille.

"Cam, could you see if Greg needs help?" Obviously, Rose didn't want him sticking around. To the Dean boys, she asked, "Can I get either of you a cup of coffee? If you'd like a meal, the grill is still hot."

"No, nothing for us. We won't be long." Karl followed Rose to a table in front and sat down.

Cam waited a moment longer, but Rose didn't glance his way. He entered the kitchen filled with the rattling sounds of Greg loading up the industrial dishwasher.

"Can I help?"

"Yeah." Greg grinned and then nodded toward the diner. "Who are those guys?"

"Linda Dean's sons Kory and Karl."

The kid's eyes grew round as a pair of bobbers. "Really? They're my uncles." He ran for the doorway and peeked out. "What do they want?"

"To talk to your mom. Haven't you met them before?"

Greg shook his head, but continued to stare into the diner. "Nope. Never."

Cam frowned. Evidently, Rose had married the oldest, Kurt Dean. Hadn't she been welcomed into the Dean family? If that were true, then why had Linda left her the diner? Karl and Kory obviously didn't know her. Rose must not have attended Linda's funeral and clearly, Karl and Kory hadn't been to Rose and Kurt's wedding.

He glanced at Greg watching the Deans with wistful eyes, and his gut twisted. He knew that wish-filled feeling running through the kid. Wishing for things that couldn't be or hadn't been.

Cam wished he read more easily. He wished he hadn't been disqualified at last year's fishing tournament. He wished he hadn't lost every last one of his sponsors because of it. He wished he could turn back the clock and do things differently. He had only today and all his tomorrows to make things right.

"Greg, honey, can you come out here?" Rose called to her son, hating the way her voice cracked.

"No need, Rose. We don't need to meet your boy." Karl got up from the table.

Rose stood, meeting Karl's gaze directly even though her knees might give out at any moment. "He's Kurt's boy, too, and that makes him your nephew. My hope is to pass this diner on to him. It's what Linda intended."

The two brothers shared a look, then Kory spread his hands wide. "We're just trying to help you out."

She didn't buy it. Not for a second. "Then why are you trying to take the diner away me?"

"We're willing to pay—"

Greg came out from the kitchen and stood next to her. "Yeah?"

"Greg, these are your uncles. Kory and Karl Dean." Rose stood straighter when her son reached out for a handshake like the properly raised young man he was. She wanted them to see Greg's face. He looked so much like Kurt, their brother. Karl and Kory were taking from blood, threatening their own family.

"Hello."

"Greg." Karl briefly shook hands, followed by Kory. Neither man met her son's eyes. "Rose, you've got a week to decide."

Shame on them! She stood ramrod straight until they unlocked the front door and walked out of the diner. Then she crumpled into a chair.

"Mom! You okay?"

"Yes." She sounded weary, even to her own ears.

Cam came out from the kitchen, looking concerned. "Greg, will you do me a favor and grab three beef patties from the fridge and throw them on the grill?"

Greg didn't move.

Rose hated to see the worried look on her son's face and smiled. "Go ahead, honey. We might as well have lunch before meeting Grandma and Grandpa."

Cam locked the front door and returned. "What was that all about?"

Rose needed to unload before she saw her parents and fell apart. They had texted her before the Deans came in that they were getting settled into a hotel room in the larger town across the bay. She didn't want to add to their worries about her. Looking up at Cam, she didn't have time to be choosy. If she didn't air this one out, she'd cry.

Rose hated to cry, so she gave way to anger. "They are threatening to contest Linda's will if I don't agree to a buyout of the diner."

Cam whistled.

"Yeah. And I have a week to decide." Rose threw her head back and stared at the ceiling, willing those unshed tears to stay put.

"Mom?" Greg sounded scared.

"It's okay, honey. Just some business with the diner. Help Cam make lunch, okay?"

"I'm not a baby. You can tell me."

Rose sighed. "Greg—"

Cam turned to her son. "Got those patties on the grill?"

"Yup." Greg crossed his arms, refusing to move.

Cam placed a hand on Greg's shoulder. "Let's get the rest of the stuff we need and then we can talk while we eat."

Greg looked ready to argue but glanced at her for direction.

"Go ahead with Cam. I'll get us each a pop and we can sit at the counter." Rose dragged herself out of the chair and headed for the soft-drink dispenser. She grabbed three plastic tumblers stacked on the shelf below and filled them halfway with ice followed by cola for her and root beer for her son. She didn't know what Cam liked. "What kind of pop do you want?"

He shrugged as he flipped each burger. "Doesn't matter."

"Are you going to tell me, Mom?"

Rose looked at Cam. He didn't look back and concentrated on placing a slice of cheddar on each burger. She faced her son. "Your uncles want to buy the diner."

"But we just got it." Greg's voice rose.

"I know."

"Will we move back home?"

She watched Cam construct each cheeseburger on the plates. He was clearly staying out of the conversation. As he should, but then Rose realized she'd raised her son's hopes by keeping quiet on the Dean boys' threat. "I don't want to sell, Greg. I'd like to have something that's ours. Yours and mine. Something you can take over after college."

Greg mulled what she'd said. "What if I don't want it?"

Rose chose her words carefully. "We can cross that bridge when we get there. For now, I like being my own boss. Here, I have more time with you."

Greg shifted. "Awww, Mom…"

"It's time we make our own home." Furious for having to talk her son into this all over again, Rose quickly changed the subject. "Greg, will you grab the bag of chips in back? Cam's got our burgers done."

"K."

When Greg walked away, Cam looked her in the eyes. "This diner might be worth more than you think. Maybe you should talk to Linda's attorney, get his thoughts about today's events. He's right here in Maple Springs."

"I can't afford an attorney," she hissed.

"You might not have a choice."

Rose hated that he was probably right.

Greg tossed the bag of chips on the counter and sat on one of the stools and spun around a couple of times.

"Three cheeseburgers." Cam set down three plates.

Rose wasn't in the mood to eat, but took a bite anyway. The burgers were sloppy, stacked with lettuce and tomato and pickles. Perfect.

"Aren't we going to pray?" Greg challenged her. He did that a lot lately.

She nodded, her mouth full.

Cam cleared his throat. "I'll pray."

Her gaze flew to Cam, but he'd already bowed his head. She did the same while he recited a formal-sounding prayer.

"Bless us, oh Lord, and these Thy gifts..."

Her mind wandered. She didn't want to sell.

The deed hadn't even transferred to her yet, so how could she sell?

"Which we are about to receive, from Thy bounty..."

But then, what if Karl and Kory contested the will and she lost? She'd have nothing. No legacy for Greg. Nothing.

"Through Christ, Our Lord. Amen."

She felt a warm, large hand cover hers. Startled, her eyes flew open and locked with Cam's. He looked kind and genuine.

His hand remained on hers. "How'd you find out that you'd inherited the diner?"

Rose slid her hand back and tried to think. She'd met this man only a few hours ago. Even though he'd helped her when things had gone from bad to worse, she shouldn't trust him. Still, it'd be nice to unload on someone other than her parents. They worried about her enough as it was. "Um, I received a letter enclosed in a packet that I had to sign for. Would you like to read it?"

"Uh...sure."

Rose popped off the stool and darted upstairs, returning in moments with a fat folder. Rifling through the financials that had been sent, as well, Rose pulled out the letter and handed it to Cam.

His gazed raked over the document as he chewed, then he waved it away. "Why don't you read it?"

Rose glanced at Greg. Her son nodded in agreement as he took the last bite of his cheeseburger. She slid her plate toward him. "You can have mine."

Greg reached for her sandwich with only two bites taken. "Mmm, yeah."

Rose made the mistake of looking back at Cam. Gazing into those brilliant blue eyes full of concern brought a hitch in her breathing. Now was not the time to fall apart. Taking a deep breath, Rose rallied her strength and read.

"'I am hereby writing to inform you that the inheritance process has been successfully completed and the will of Linda M. Dean has been put into action. According to said will, Rose Dean will immediately inherit the business titled Dean's Hometown Grille and the commercial building therein at the bequest left by Linda M. Dean to you.'"

Rose lowered the letter. "Then there's the stuff about transference of property and Linda's wish for Greg to eventually take over. Financials were also included in the package."

"Sounds legit," Cam finally said.

"Well, yeah. Why wouldn't it be?"

"I don't know." Cam gestured to the packet. "So all that came with the letter?"

Rose nodded and pushed the folder toward Cam. "Three years' worth of business tax returns."

"Have you looked at them?"

Rose shook her head. She'd never been good with that sort of thing. She couldn't even figure out her own tax returns let alone a business like this one. "I don't know what to look for."

Cam pushed his plate out of the way. "Greg, would you mind taking the dishes to the kitchen? I'd like to talk to your mom a minute."

Greg looked at her.

Rose nodded. "I got these. Why don't you go upstairs and clean up."

Greg slid off the stool, but he gathered up the empty plates anyway. "Thanks, Cam. The burgers were really good."

"You're welcome." After her boy entered the kitchen, he added, "You've done a good job. He's a good kid."

"Thanks. My parents helped, especially my dad." She searched Cam's face. "What am I going to do?"

"To my knowledge, the Deans live downstate and have never been involved in the diner. My guess is that they think you're sitting on a gold mine. You need to find out if that's true in those financials."

"I can't afford an accountant and even if I could, would he have the answer in a week?"

"I can take a look."

Rose stared at him. "You know what to look for?"

Cam nodded. "I know how to find a business's cash flow. I've kept track of my own and double-checked my business manager's figures."

Cam had a business manager? Rose wrestled with that bit of information. What exactly did this man do for a living?

"Rose, you can trust me."

He'd misunderstood her silence. But trust wasn't something she should hand over along with her financials. Drumming her fingertips on the laminate countertop, Rose had an idea. Hopefully a good one. "Okay. You can look them over on one condition."

He narrowed his eyes. "What's that?"

"You have to teach me how to figure them out, too."

Cam smiled, broad and sure. "Done. We can get started right now if you'd like."

Rose stood and gathered up her packet of information. "I can't. My parents are up for the weekend."

"How about Monday? After we close the diner." Cam stood, too. "I've worked in restaurants on and off since I was a kid. I can fill in for a few days."

Rose ignored the flutter of nerves hearing them described as *we* but she didn't have many options. She didn't have much time, either. Squaring her shoulders, she agreed. "Monday, after we close."

Her future and Greg's legacy depended on this. Rose needed all the facts before seeking out Linda's attorney. Time wasn't on her side and Cam might be her only hope. He was also an attractive man. One she knew little about. If this was some sort of game for him, a way to come on to her, he could prove to be her biggest fear.

Chapter Two

"Oh, Rose, this is lovely!" Her mother looked around, smiling as she entered the diner. Her parents had showed up sooner than expected. "Your father is parking the car. This is so nostalgic with the red vinyl chairs and spinning stools. I love it."

"I'm glad." Rose gave her mom a big hug.

Many told Rose that she resembled her mom. They shared the same eye color and clothing size and practice of dyeing their hair. Although, her mom covered gray with a light brown shade; Rose used her naturally mousy color to hide. She didn't care to be noticed, especially by men. Once upon a time, Rose had experimented with more striking shades for the fun of it. Not now. Everything she did had to have a bigger reason, a purpose.

The rattle of pots and pans sounded from the kitchen. Her mom craned her neck to see. "Is that Greg?"

"He's upstairs getting cleaned up. That's our cook." Rose hesitated. Cam was only filling in, but she didn't want her folks to know about all the drama today.

Her mom frowned. "We came too early."

"Not at all." Rose had finished wiping down the tables and chairs while Cam cleaned up the prep station and last bit of the kitchen.

Her father tapped at the front door.

Rose waved him in and gave him a hug. "Thanks for coming."

Her father gave her an extra squeeze before letting go. "We had to see where you were and this is quite a place you've got here."

"Grandpa!" Greg charged straight for him.

"Heyyyyy." Her father enveloped her son in a bear hug.

Watching them, Rose swallowed the lump lodged in her throat and turned to lock the front door. She and Greg hadn't been here a month, yet it seemed much longer. Maybe accepting the Deans' offer would give her enough for Greg's college fund if she put it all away. Maybe she should play it safe and not risk her son's future. Greg might be better off near her dad facing the high school years.

Maybe her dreams should wait.

"Rose, I'm taking off." Cam stood in the kitchen doorway.

Thoughts scattered and she momentarily stared. "Yeah, okay."

Cam stared back. "I'll see you Monday."

His tousled hair curled from the steam of washing the remaining dishes. The front of his shirt showed water spots, as well. Why did he have to look so good? "Thanks for everything."

Her mother stepped forward. "You're the cook?"

"That's Cam," Greg volunteered. "He took over after Chuck quit right in the middle of lunchtime."

Too late, Rose couldn't shush her son from letting that news out of the bag.

Her mom cast her a worried frown before extending her hand toward Cam. "I'm Louise, but my friends call me Lou. And this is my husband, Frank."

"My parents." Rose pointed out the obvious.

Cam shook first her mother's hand and then her father's, giving them that gleaming smile of his. "Nice to meet you both."

"So, what happened?"

"Mom, I'll tell you later. I'm sure Cam wants to leave." She gave him a pointed look. She didn't need her folks knowing anything but the positive stuff.

"Right, okay then." Cam hesitated.

Her mom's gaze swung from Cam back to her. Greg kept going. "Chuck got mad at Mom and quit. Cam was in here eating lunch and he just started cooking. It was great."

"I'm filling in until Rose finds someone permanent."

"I see." Her mom's eyes narrowed. "Thank you for helping Rose."

"He makes the best cheeseburgers," Greg said. "Way better than Chuck."

"Not better than mine." Her dad ruffled her son's hair.

"I don't know, Gramps. They're pretty good."

"Thanks, buddy." Cam fist-bumped her son's ready hand. "I really do need to leave, though. Very nice to meet you both."

"See ya, Cam." Greg grinned.

They watched him leave, and Rose braced for the inevitable questions.

"Is that true? He just got up and helped out? Who is this guy?" Her father beat out her mom.

"His name is Cam Zelinsky. He grew up here and he's got restaurant experience."

"Doesn't he have another job?" her mom added.

Rose sighed. She didn't know exactly. She was placing the future of her diner in a stranger's hands reviewing those tax returns. "He owns his own business, but I'm not sure what. I'll find out more next week."

"Hmm."

Rose could see the gears turning inside her

mother's head. "Come up and see the apartment. I'll change and then we can go for a walk around town."

Her mom kept pace with her while Greg and her father dawdled, looking over the diner more closely.

Rose paused, in case there was something on his mind, but her father was looking at a grouping of framed vintage postcards that depicted Maple Springs around the turn of the century. Even then, this area had lured folks from downstate for the pristine summer months.

"Greg sure seems to like this Cam fellow," her mom whispered.

"Mom..." Rose knew where this was headed and slammed on the brakes. "We met him today. Please, don't even go there."

"What?" Her mother tipped her head. "Why not?"

"Because." Rose kept walking.

Her mother knew better than anyone the heartache she'd gone through when Greg had turned four. That's when Kurt had served her divorce papers and Rose had been a mess. Her mom had urged Rose to move back home, so she did. Her mother had watched Greg while Rose worked erratic restaurant hours waitressing. In time, she'd been promoted to waitstaff supervisor and then finally she'd landed an events manager position. Her parents had been the anchor she'd needed after being set adrift by her husband.

The sad thing was that even after a failed marriage and her last dating disaster, her mother still wanted to see her only daughter walk down the aisle. Rose had robbed her parents of a wedding day when she'd eloped with Kurt. They'd been disappointed for sure, but adamant that she stay in college. She'd let them down on that one, too.

Rose sighed.

"Tired, honey?" Her mom followed her up the steps that led to the apartment over the diner.

Her father and Greg had caught up to them and four sets of feet stomped up the narrow wooden stairwell.

"A little." Rose was more scared than weary.

Aside from a few months of college, she was truly on her own for the first time in her life. Part of her wanted to run back to the comfort of living with her parents, but God had given her this opportunity.

Linda's sons had thrown her off balance today with their threat to take her inheritance away. Linda's will had been so clear; at least that's the way it had sounded from the packet she'd received.

Once Rose understood those financials, she'd have a better reference point to consider whether the Deans' offer was a good one. After all, knowledge was power. She hoped Cam knew what he was doing and she prayed he wasn't playing her.

What was he doing?

Cam stared at the flames licking the dry tinder he'd helped his father stack into the fire pit. It might not have cooled off enough to need a campfire, but what was a summer's eve gathering without one?

Seriously, what made him think he could teach Rose to read her business returns? *Read.* Ha! That was an odd choice of terms considering his issues with written words. Numbers were different. Numbers were concrete and made sense, like that periodic table.

"You can toss that log on now." His father touched his shoulder. "Cam?"

"Huh? Oh." He tossed in the piece of wood he'd held and then reached for another.

"You okay, son?"

"Yeah, sure." He'd escaped from the noise of the back deck to help his father while everyone else cleaned up after dinner.

In honor of Father's Day, his mom had gathered his siblings for a cookout. Matthew was out on the Great Lakes with his job as a freighter first mate, but his wife, Annie, and her baby, John, were here. Zach and his fiancée, Ginger. Even Darren, although he'd sulked through dinner, since his girlfriend had recently left for her music thing in Seattle. Of course Monica, his younger brothers—Ben, Marcus and Luke—and their baby sister, Erin, were here, too. His sister Cat, working on assignment somewhere, was also absent.

"Something on your mind then?"

Cam looked his dad in the eye. Retired from a long army career, Andrew Zelinsky still carried an air of authority that encouraged the truth or else. As usual, Cam darted around giving a straight answer. "I'll figure it out."

"No word on a new sponsor."

"Not yet."

"What's past is past." His father nodded. "You'll make a comeback."

"Right." Cam snorted and stared at those flames some more.

He'd leveled with his folks to an extent. He'd been disqualified from a tournament last year because he'd broken practice rules by fishing after dark. He'd broken more than that with an illegal catch, but nothing had been proven. Still, that decision had not only dropped his standings to the bottom of the pile, but cost him his last sponsor. It could have been worse. He could have been banned from the profession and it would have been justified. Although rumors swirled, his business manager had been able to keep things relatively quiet.

Still, Cam had pushed things far too many times in his fishing career. When competition got fierce and the stakes were high, he'd cut corners. Literally. He'd trimmed fins on fish to make sure they qualified. He'd even stuffed a couple lead sinkers into the bellies of bass for better weigh-ins.

Cam had massaged the truth so well that he'd gotten away with it too many times. It had finally cost him, though. Like now, offering to teach Rose how to review her financials when he only knew what the numbers meant and where they should be.

"How's the *new job*?" Monica wiggled her eyebrows at him with a teasing glint in her eyes.

Relieved for an escape from his father's scrutiny, Cam laughed. "I'm just filling in."

"I can't believe you're cooking at my favorite place to eat. Don't mess with it too much." His brother Darren pulled a soft drink can out of an ice-packed metal tub and cracked the tab.

"Come by and see." Cam tossed another log on the fire, grabbed an icy beverage and kept staring into the flames.

"I don't get it, why are you working there? If you need money—"

"The new owner is pretty and single," Monica pointed out.

"Ahh." Darren nodded. "Now it all makes sense."

Cam took a long drink and shrugged. "She

needed help and I've got a few days before fishing in the first Northern Open."

"So, you swooped right in and saved the day."

"It's what I do." Cam winked.

"Poor woman. Does she know about you?"

"Not yet." Cam laughed, but his brother didn't realize just how loaded his teasing words were.

"I'm hearing good things about Rose Dean. The women on the church planning committee are looking for a place to have their meeting. I'll tell them to go there." His mom wrapped an arm around his waist and gave him a squeeze.

"Thanks, Mom." Grateful for the switched focus, Cam scratched his forehead.

"Is everything all set for the Fourth of July barbecue?" Monica asked. "It's only two weeks away and I need to print off the flyers."

"It's a go." His mother looked up at him. "Would you be interested in grilling? It's going to be big this year. The chamber is sponsoring a live band for entertainment complete with a dance floor."

"Nope." Cam backed away from his mom and slid onto a lounge chair. He took a long pull from his drink. If he fished well at the tournament the weekend before the Fourth, any number of opportunities could arise and Cam wanted to be ready to accept.

Darren raised his hands. "Don't look at me. I'm on duty that day."

Cam watched their mom wrangle their younger brothers into manning the huge grills for their church's biggest fund-raiser. Ignoring the stitch of guilt that tweaked for not helping, Cam figured he'd buy a ticket instead. Maybe two or three, enough to take Rose and Greg, if he was around.

No matter how attractive he found Rose Dean, Cam knew better than to ask her for a real date. Romancing Rose would be like walking into quicksand. Not only was there a kid involved, but Cam didn't do anything long-term. Fishing came first and fishing kept him traveling. It wasn't only his livelihood, it was his life. It's all he had and he'd come too close to ruining it for good.

Going to the Fourth of July barbecue would be about introducing Rose to more folks in town. Establishing her as the new owner of the Grille and proving she belonged there. He didn't want those Dean boys getting their hands on the diner. Not when Linda had wanted Rose to have it. Not when Rose wanted it. Whatever it took, he'd help her keep it.

Monday morning, Rose entered the diner a little before six in the morning. The early sun shone on a quiet Main Street, making the overnight dew glisten. It was so quiet this morning, she hated to ruin it. But she had a business to run and dropped whole roasted coffee beans into the large grinder and pressed the button. She ignored the teeth-jarring sound and savored the rich smell of fresh ground coffee. Would Cam be late? He knew the diner opened at seven, but they hadn't talked about when he should arrive.

A rap at the door startled her. Cam peered through the front door glass waiting for her to let him in. The sun hit him from behind, making the ends of his blond hair shine like gold. He wore khaki shorts and a T-shirt and a colorful bandanna over his head like a cap.

Her mouth dropped open, so she closed it quick. "You're early."

"Good morning to you, too. Haven't you ever heard the early bird gets the worm? Believe it or not, I've always been a morning person." He winked at her.

Rose felt her cheeks heat and looked down, spotting a brand new six-pack of tall glass tumblers in his hand. "What are those for?"

"Iced tea. I like my iced tea in real glass." Cam headed for the kitchen like he owned the place. "Any specials today?"

Rose hadn't thought that far. Chuck had always been the one to decide which specials to make. "You choose."

He opened the industrial fridge and grinned. It was the same good-time smile he'd given her before. "I'll see what you've got."

Rose ignored the swirling butterflies that raucous grin produced and followed him. "There's a load of whitefish in the freezer Chuck was supposed to do something with."

Cam grabbed a small metal cart with shelves and loaded it up with things needed for the prep station. She'd had her doubts but this morning, Cam eased them. He definitely knew his way around a restaurant.

Rose relaxed. "Coffee's done, would you like a cup?"

Cam didn't even look up from the depths of the fridge. "Yeah. Light cream and sugar."

Rose fixed them each a mug. Easy, since they drank their coffee the same way. She offered a steaming cup to Cam as he filled the prep station with the items from the cart. "Here."

"Thanks." He accepted it, took a sip and then looked at her. "It's good."

"Hey, I want to thank you for all this."

Cam nodded. "You're welcome."

"You said you've done this before?"

He grabbed a metal mixing bowl and the muscles of his arms flexed. "From low-end to high-end, I've worked in a lot of restaurants. I used to wait tables at the Maple Springs Inn during my high school years. So, how do you fit into the Deans? You married Linda's eldest son, right?"

Rose sighed. "Yes. I was married to Kurt."

Cam looked concerned. "I read about Kurt's death in a tour bus accident a few years ago. Then Linda—man, I'm sorry for your losses."

Rose had lost a mother-in-law she barely knew and an ex-husband she'd rather forget. She'd lost her husband years before his death, before his career really took off, but Cam didn't need to know all that. "Thank you."

Cam's intent gaze studied her. "I can fill in for Chuck until he comes back."

"But don't you have another job, your own business perhaps?"

Cam's bright eyes dimmed. "Not for a little while."

Rose scrunched her nose. What did that mean? "I'll pay you the same rate as Chuck. He was paid pretty well, but I don't want him back. I've already emailed the newspaper to run an ad for a new cook."

He nodded as if the money didn't matter. "That's fine."

Rose went to grab the new hire paperwork from a small file cabinet under the cash register stand. She hadn't even checked him out, references and the like. What if— No, he'd proven himself capable. "If you wouldn't mind filling out your information and the W-4, I'll place you on the payroll effective this past Saturday."

"Okay." Cam took the forms and pen she offered. It didn't take long before he handed them back.

Rose glanced over everything. Cam's handwriting was atrocious. "So, what is it that you normally do?"

"Does it matter?"

Rose felt her stomach clench. "It might."

Leaning against the counter, Cam folded his arms, which were already nicely browned from the sun. Those pesky muscles of his flexed again, too. "I'm a professional fisherman."

Had she heard correctly? "As in like a charter boat or guide?"

His lips formed a grim line for only a moment, then that flirty grin returned. "As in the Bass Pro circuit. I'm heading for a qualifying tournament this upcoming weekend, so I can cook for the next few days until you find someone permanent."

"Oh." She wasn't sure what that meant, but it sounded an awful lot like something her ex-husband used to say when he was between music gigs.

"It's none of my business, but is it only you and your son working here?"

Rose nodded. "After Linda died and the diner closed for a bit, the waitress she had went to another job. I just hired a replacement. She and a busboy both start later this morning. I enrolled

Greg in a summer program that goes from eleven to four. Today is his first day."

"My church has a summer teen program. If it's the same, Greg's in good hands. They do a lot."

Cam went to church? He'd prayed over their food Saturday, but it was a rote prayer. Rose narrowed her gaze. "What church do you attend?"

"The big white one at the end of Main, the other side of Center Park. Can't miss it."

Rose knew exactly where he meant. The structure was Christmas-card beautiful as well as a traditional denomination she didn't belong to. Looking into Cam's blue eyes, she wondered where he was coming from. Nobody did something this big out of the goodness of their hearts without wanting something in return.

He went to church.

Anyone could attend a church. What really mattered was where a person placed God in their lives. "Why are you doing this?"

Cam shrugged. "Let's just say I'm trying to be a better person."

Rose didn't like the sound of that, either. What had he done to make him need redemption? With his looks and lazy smiles, she could only imagine. She might find Cam attractive, but she wasn't stupid, nor would she allow herself to become interested. Rose wanted to keep the vow she'd made not to date until after Greg was grown and gone off to college. She'd be older and hopefully wiser by then.

Her husband had walked out on her and their four-year-old son. The next man she'd offered her heart to had crushed it. He'd turned out to be a fraud with no genuine interest in Greg. Her son had been only eight at the time. Old enough to have his heart trampled, too.

Soon after, they got word that Kurt had died.

Nope, Rose had been burned well enough to know not to misplace her trust ever again. Staring Cam down, she weighed her options and didn't have any. She needed a cook and he'd offered to fill the gap, for a few days anyway. "We've got a deal then."

"Yes, we do, Rose." Cam gave her that lazy smile. "Now, I've got a special of the day to plan."

"Yes, you do." Rose watched him return to the kitchen before settling on the stool near her cash register with her tablet.

She didn't like the way he'd spoken her name like a caress. No wait, she *did* like it, and that was the problem. She refused to be putty in anyone's hands. If he expected her to fawn over him, he was wasting all that charm.

Professional fisherman. Ha!

The lines around Cam's eyes hinted that he had to be close to her age of just over thirty, but he seemed like a big kid at heart. What kind of career could someone really have fishing? The image of Huckleberry Finn came to mind and Rose nearly giggled.

Cam was a character, all right, but men like him and her ex-husband were all too common. They didn't want to grow up and certainly wouldn't live up to their responsibilities. Her ex had barely paid his child support and that had been the extent of his fatherly duty. The last time Kurt had seen his own son had been after Greg had turned six. Kurt had shown up with a sorry excuse for missing their child's birthday.

She heard the rattle of the metal cart being pushed to the prep station once again and took in the items on top. The frozen whitefish, potatoes, cabbage, raisins, almonds, lemons and sweet pickle relish.

Curious, she got up and went toward him. "What do you have in mind for today's special?"

Cam's blue eyes gleamed. "I have that whitefish you mentioned. I'm thinking fish and chips with a side of kicked up coleslaw."

"Kicked up?"

He winked. "You'll see."

Rose ignored the flutter in her belly. "I've some paperwork to do before we open. Let me know if you need anything."

"Will do."

Rose returned to her spot by the cash register. She had a bar stool and her tablet for inputting sales into a rudimentary spreadsheet. She'd never owned a business before but keeping track of income and expenses seemed like a good start.

She caught the sound of Cam's humming as he worked getting the two fryers heated up. It sounded familiar, but she couldn't place the tune. Cam had a deep tone to his voice that was definitely distracting. She'd get nothing done if she didn't stop noticing every little thing about him.

"There's a radio on the shelf, if you need music. I usually play the country station." It's the music she'd been around most of her adult life. The radio wouldn't pull at her like Cam.

"Maybe later." He continued to hum.

She couldn't stand it. The familiarity of the song remained out of reach over the sounds of metal spoon scraping metal mixing bowl. "What's that you're humming?"

He shrugged. "I don't know the name, but I heard it on the Christian radio station, about the Cross."

"As in Calvary?"

He looked confused. "As in Crucifixion."

Rose nodded. Her church lingo might be different than his, but he seemed to be a genuine believer. Concentrating on entering the previous day's receipts, she didn't notice Cam's approach until she sensed him standing beside her.

"Try this." He held out a forkful of creamy, golden-colored coleslaw toward her.

She went for the fork, but he pulled away slightly with a teasing look in his eye. "I've got it, just take a bite."

Rose wished he'd back up a little. Standing this close, she could smell him, and Cam smelled nice. Over the tangy coleslaw, Rose detected a crisp, clean lemony scent that tempted her to inhale far deeper than she should. She looked at the forkful and then up into his eyes.

Big mistake. He had that flirty, good-time smile going again.

She tasted the slaw. Very creamy and sweet with a hint of something she couldn't name— "Is that curry?"

He nodded. "Very good and yes, it is. I prefer dates, but raisins work well in a pinch."

Rose smiled at him—a little stunned, a little thrown off guard and a whole lot grateful. Cam might be the best cook this diner had ever seen. "That's really good."

"I know. Want me to get the door?"

Rose checked her watch. Five minutes to seven. She slid off her stool, grabbed her checkered apron and headed for the front. "I got it. You do your thing." Then she stopped and turned. "Cam?"

"Yeah?" Wearing that silly bandanna, he looked like a rescuing swashbuckler off the pages of one of her childhood books. No black patch, but his longish blond hair with ends that tended to curl and those piercing blue eyes nailed the descriptive. He might wield a spoon instead of a gleaming sword, but he'd saved her from a big headache. He'd saved the diner, too.

She needed to get those fairy-tale images out of her head and fast before they swept her away. "Thank you."

He gave her a pleased smile. "You're welcome, Rose."

She grit her teeth at the sound of her name on his lips and headed for the front door. The man knew how to make her head spin. Heart pounding, Rose kicked herself as a fool.

Why did she do this? Why did she always cast a man who showed a speck of interest in helping her into the knight-in-shining armor role? She had learned the hard way that every one of her past *knights* had proven themselves tarnished and lacking in honor.

She'd inherited a diner and although she'd been in the foodservice business for years, ownership scared her. Cam's charm scared her, too. Men like Cam couldn't be trusted and Rose needed to keep that at the forefront of her mind. His employment was temporary. Everything about Cam screamed temporary and irresponsible.

A man better left alone.

Chapter Three

By 2:05, the diner was empty save for her, Cam and Jess, the pretty new waitress who had started this morning, along with the new busboy named Chris.

Rose locked the front door and flipped over her sign. "Phew, busy day."

"I've seen worse." Jess grinned. She'd held her own today.

Rose smiled back. The girl was nice, cheeky but respectful, even toward Cam. Especially toward Cam. "You did well today. Thanks for your help."

Jess lifted her wad of tip money. "Not bad for a Monday. I can't wait to see what the weekend brings."

"Not bad at all." Rose had never seen so many receipts skewered onto the check spindle by the cash register.

The two of them had quickly turned over tables,

keeping the busboy busy. Chris clanged around in the kitchen, loading dishes in racks that rolled through an industrial dishwasher. The kid had done a good job today, too. Rose had him only through the summer until he returned to high school in the fall.

Rose itched to get at those financials, but that would have to keep until after cleanup.

"I'll see you tomorrow." Jess waved and then yelled out to Cam, who was busy breaking down his prep station.

"See ya, kid."

Rose chuckled as she headed for the kitchen. Cam didn't flirt with Jess. He'd joked around, but that was it. No good-time smiles and a good thing, too. Jess wasn't yet out of her teens.

Rose had been only eighteen when she'd met a twenty-five-year-old Kurt Dean. He'd swept her away with his artistic dreams and careless good looks. Kurt hadn't been old by any means, but certainly old enough to know better than to fill a young girl's head with promises he never intended to keep.

"Need help in here?" Cam's voice sounded close behind her.

She'd been standing in the entryway lost in thought and didn't hear his approach. Rose could feel his warmth behind her and quickly stepped away. "Chris has it under control, but thank you."

"Any word on a cook?"

Rose shook her head. She'd placed the advertisement only this morning. "No. Nothing yet."

A slow smile spread across his handsome face. "I'll help you interview if you get any hits this week."

"Thanks. That'd be great." Rose carried her bucket of soapy bleach water with her to wipe down the tables and chairs.

Cam was a good diner cook. He'd waited on folks seated at the counter while she and Jess had been busy. Where would she find his equal let alone a replacement by the week's end?

It was nearly two thirty when they'd finished cleaning up and Chris clocked out. Rose turned toward Cam. They had an hour and a half before Greg came home. "I'll grab those financials."

"Sure. I'll be in the dining area." Cam nodded.

Rose scurried up the stairs to the roasting apartment above the diner. It might not be the ideal living situation, with only one small bedroom that she'd given to Greg, but it had come with the building she'd inherited along with the business. She was determined to make do until she knew what kind of income to expect after a year or so.

When she returned to the coolness of the air-conditioned diner, even with the lights off, there was plenty of sunlight streaming in through the plate glass window facing Main. Before Rose joined Cam at the table in the sunniest spot, she asked, "Want something to drink?"

"No." Cam pulled off the bandanna and finger combed his mop of thick blond hair. "Look, Rose, I'm no accountant. I can only tell you what I see."

"I understand." He'd already gone above and beyond and was even now, off the clock helping her. "Whatever you teach me will be a big help and much appreciated."

"Yeah? How much?" He grinned at her, teasing. It wasn't the good-time look he'd first given her, but softer. More like the kind of smile a kid might follow up with *What will you give me?*

Rose laughed.

"I see you're not taking me seriously." Cam pulled the manila envelope close and emptied the contents, then he winked at her.

She ignored the erratic dance of her pulse and watched as he spread the stack of paperwork out and thumbed through the pages. Her heart sank when he didn't say anything for quite some time. "Well?"

Cam leaned back and sighed. "The Grille has made a profit each of these three years, but the most recent one saw a slight increase."

"And the bad news?"

Cam shrugged. "There isn't any that I can see."

Rose pulled the paperwork closer and zeroed in on the first page and a line called Ordinary

Business Income. "It sure doesn't look like that big a profit."

"That's not the whole picture." Cam flipped further into the packet and pointed. "This schedule is pretty much a balance sheet. There's no paper losses or depreciation deductions here. This shows real dollars. Cash at the beginning of the year, cash at the end, and how that cash is used. These payments by the business are more than likely rent paid to Linda."

"But it was all hers. Why pay rent to herself?"

Cam chuckled. "In a nutshell, The Grille paid Linda rent to help decrease its taxable income."

"Oh." Amazed, Rose stared at him. "How come you know so much about this stuff if you're a fisherman?"

He looked surprised, as if he wasn't used to such a compliment. "Even though I have my taxes done, I still review both my personal and business returns to make sure they're correct. I keep track of my income and expenses throughout the year and always have."

"Smart." Rose nodded. Considering the scope of not only owning the diner, but the building, too, she needed to hire an accountant and soon. "So, based on what you see, am I sitting on a gold mine?"

"Not quite, but I think you inherited a good

business and, with the right people, you can increase profits."

He was one of those right people. He not only
made super-tasty food, but he was good with the
customers. He welcomed the volume instead of
cursing it like Chuck had. Having grown up here,
Cam knew everybody and greeted them by name.
The dining patrons loved seeing Cam at the grill,
too.

"You'd really help me interview cooks?"

He gave her a slow smile. "And transition them,
if I can."

"But you're only here for a few more days."

"I won't leave you hanging, Rose."

She searched his gaze, wanting to believe him,
not knowing how he could possibly deliver when
he was leaving at the end of the week.

He pointed at the bottom of the first page,
bringing her attention back to the books. "Based
on profits, you can certainly afford to hire an accountant. This is the firm Linda used and as far
as I know, they're good."

Rose hadn't paid herself a salary other than
her tips because she'd been afraid of the immedi-
ate bills, including the cook's payroll, eating up
profits and the modest business checking account
she'd also inherited. She'd deposited all cash receipts until she figured out a budget.

"So, what do you think the Deans are after? I can't see them running this diner."

"No. I can't, either," Cam agreed. "Maybe the building? Rents are high on Main Street."

"Show me more." Rose scooted her chair closer to make it easier to see the pages. Staring at those pages, she hoped they'd uncover the motive for the Deans' threat.

Maybe then she'd know how to stop them.

Sitting this close to Rose, Cam detected a delicate fragrance. Underneath the cloying aroma of French fries and bacon grease that clung to both of them, he inhaled her soft scent. Leaning closer, he breathed deep.

She was dangerously sweet.

He appreciated the way her short hair swirled to a point at the back of her slender neck. His fingers itched to trace that hairline and see if her skin felt as soft as it looked.

Rose leaned back. "Okay, so you were saying?"

What was he saying? "Ummm, yeah."

"Earth to Cam." She laughed, having no clue that he'd been checking her out.

He rubbed the bridge of his nose.

Rose immediately looked repentant. "I'm sorry, it's been a long day and you're tired. We can do this another time."

He didn't dare meet her eyes. He wasn't that tired. "It's fine. Let's see. The balance sheet—"

Rose scooped up the paperwork and stuffed it in the envelope. "Nope, this is too much for today."

He glanced at the clock reading 3:15. They'd been going over figures for nearly an hour. "How about we get some fresh air? We can walk to the beach and meet your son before the program lets out and see how he likes it. On a hot day like this, they're probably there."

"And if they're not?" Rose looked like she relished the idea but wasn't so sure of walking there with him.

"Leave a note for Greg that we'll be back."

She stared at him a moment longer and then agreed. "Okay, let me grab my keys."

The public beach wasn't far, only a couple short blocks across the street from the diner. Cam walked beside a quiet Rose. Outside the diner, she seemed tense and barely looked at him.

"Where'd you live before here?" Cam asked.

"Kalamazoo. It's where my parents live." Rose didn't embellish. She was all business, as if this wasn't a social outing.

Cam wanted to know more about her. He'd meant what he'd said about not leaving her hanging. He didn't know how he'd manage that, but it would come to him. "How do you like it here?"

"So far so good."

"It's still new." Cam chuckled. "But take a look at that lake and name a better view if you can."

Maple Bay shone turquoise near the shoreline until it blurred into a band of deep blue that touched a sunny, cloudless sky. A couple small yachts were anchored offshore.

"Beautiful, although I prefer the simple sailboats ambling in the bay instead of those big yachts."

"Crazy, isn't it? A small town like this draws people from all over in summer. Some of these yachts come from Florida, up the coast then through the lock system in New York and the Great Lakes."

"Crazy."

They slipped back into silence.

Cam searched the park and zeroed in on the far corner of the sand beach beyond the bathhouse. "The youth group is over there, playing volleyball."

"There's Greg." Rose pointed. "Can we sit here for a little bit? I don't want to interrupt the game and seem like I'm checking up on him. Even though I am."

"Sure." He waited for Rose to perch near the edge of the park bench before he sat down with plenty of room between them.

Rose turned to him, looking wary. "Why are you helping me?"

He looked out over the water and figured he'd be up-front with her. "Would you believe that I made a deal with God? I promised to be a better person if He'd give me back my livelihood."

"Give it back?"

"I lost my sponsors last year after I tanked at a big tournament." Not quite all of the truth, but enough. Cam continued, "My placements had been low for a while, and so this year I'm pretty much starting over and paying my own way. This weekend's tournament is one of three held over the next three months. I have to fish each one and end in the top five to qualify for next year's circuit. If I do well, I have a good chance of securing new sponsors who'll help fund next year and so on."

Her eyes wide, she asked, "And if you don't do well?"

"Not an option." Cam would redeem his career however long it took, even if it was the last thing he ever did.

Rose looked thoughtful. "I suppose I'd believe that, but making deals with God shouldn't be taken lightly."

Cam laughed. "You know, my mother said the same thing."

Rose frowned. "Maybe you should listen to her."

"I'm working on it." He laughed.

That much was true. He needed to change and this time he was serious. This time, he'd do things differently. He'd get it right. He'd do right instead of wrong.

He'd grown up attending church. He'd even been part of the youth group, same as the rest of his brothers and sisters, but that didn't mean the words had sunk in. The idea of eternity had been lost on him. He'd lived for the present too long and it had cost him.

Cam scanned Rose's profile. She seemed much too serious for a pretty woman with a whole lot of life left to live. He supposed losing both her husband and mother-in-law couldn't be easy on her or her son. She'd had to be tough.

He made her uncomfortable with his teasing, and yet he hadn't imagined a tug of awareness between them. He wouldn't explore it, though. Not when he needed to focus on fishing and the tournaments that kept him on the road about 70 percent of the year.

She caught him gawking. "What?"

"Does your boy like to fish?"

"I don't know."

Cam's eyebrows rose. "Didn't he ever go with his father?"

Rose's warm green eyes turned cold. "Greg was six the last time he saw his father."

That statement hit like a center punch to the gut.

Kurt Dean had died maybe three years ago, but they'd busted up long before that. Cam couldn't keep the words from falling out of his mouth. "Maybe I can take him."

"Look, Cam, I appreciate what you're trying to do. But please don't."

"Every boy needs to learn how to fish and if anyone can teach him quickly, it's me." Cam had fished from the time he could walk.

His folks still lived in the house on a small inland lake where he grew up. He'd had a Snoopy fishing pole until he turned ten and his father had given him a real, cork-handled rod like the pros used for his birthday. From then on, Cam had fished more than he did anything else.

"We're not some project for you to feel better about *your* life."

Cam hadn't meant it that quite that way. Rose hid some deep hurts and rocky bitterness and it was small wonder. Kurt Dean had abandoned them.

Rose stood. "It looks like the game is over. I'm going over there."

"Mom," Greg called out and waved.

She waved back and walked toward him.

Cam followed.

At least he could introduce her to the youth director, who happened to be his cousin. If nothing else, he could rely on John to say something

good about him. He wanted Rose to trust him. He
meant what he said about being a better person
and part of that included helping her and her son.
Whether she wanted him to or not.

Chapter Four

～

Rose walked toward the volleyball net set up on the beach. The foamy plastic clogs she wore filled with warm sand. When was the last time she'd even been to a beach? Maybe this upcoming Sunday, if the weather held, she and Greg could make a day of it here. She'd even pack a picnic lunch.

"Hey, Mom, I'm going for a swim with the others, okay?" Greg ran toward her, smiling. His eagerness was a good sign that he liked the program.

Before she could answer, her son ran into the water and dove straight under, following in the wake of a couple of other boys his age. "Well, yeah, go ahead."

"Maybe we should join them," Cam whispered close to her ear.

"No. No way." Rose ignored the little voice inside that disagreed with her quick refusal. The old

Rose would have jumped in without a thought to a towel or the fact that she wore jeans and a T-shirt.

"Hi, Cam." The youth director's smile was wide and welcoming.

"John, this is Rose Dean. Her son is Greg Dean. They're new to the area."

John extended his hand to her. "Right. New owner of Dean's Hometown Grille. You must have met with my wife when you signed up Greg. He's a good kid."

"Thank you." Rose kept her eye on her son splashing with the other kids.

"There's two lifeguards on duty. One on the beach and one on the raft out there. Is Greg a good swimmer?"

Rose bit her bottom lip. She'd enrolled him in swim lessons when he was little, but it had been ages since they'd been to any sort of pool or lake together. Greg had gone with her parents a few times near where they lived, but that had been while Rose worked. "He's passable. I think."

"He'll be fine. It's not too deep by the swim dock. Maybe seven feet. Cam and I spent many a summer on that dock." John nodded toward Cam.

Rose located Greg. He'd made it to the dock and was climbing up the ladder only to jump back in and repeat the process. "So, you've known each other a long time?"

"John's my cousin," Cam explained.

"Ah." Rose saw a faint resemblance.

"Cam was a huge help earlier this month with our canoe trip and fishing the river across the bay. This guy volunteered as if his life depended on it and I appreciated the help."

"Yeah, about that." Cam rubbed the back of his neck. "I'm pretty much tied up cooking for Rose. This week and maybe next."

Rose flashed him a look. That was news to her. He'd said he'd fill in a few days this week and she thought that would be it.

John looked at her and then back to Cam. "He's a guy of many talents."

"I'm beginning to see that," Rose agreed.

Cam laughed, but it sounded awkward and lacked conviction. "That's me."

John looked at her as he slapped Cam on the shoulder, then he checked his watch. "I've got to round up the troops before send-off. Nice to meet you, Rose."

"You, too." Rose cringed when John blew a whistle for his group to gather round.

She glanced at Cam. He'd volunteered for the youth program at his church. It was for his cousin, so maybe that didn't count. Or maybe that comment about becoming a better person was true. Cam had made a deal with God and Cam appeared to be holding up his end of the bargain.

Rose headed closer to the shoreline and waited

for Greg. "Thank you for introducing us, although I'm sure I would have met your cousin in time."

"You would have, but you're welcome anyway. I'm going in for a quick dip. You sure you don't want to join me?" He stripped off his T-shirt.

Rose did her best not to look at him and failed. Every inch of his exposed skin was golden brown. He looked like a man who didn't take life seriously. A man who had no one but himself to worry about.

She stood there like an idiot, unsure what to say or do, her face probably flaming red to boot. "Ah, no. You go ahead."

He gave her that smile. That smile that said he knew how he affected her.

She was sunk.

Greg saved the awkward moment by running toward her. "Can I go back in with Cam?"

"Come on, I'll race you to the raft." Cam waded in the water.

Greg beamed. "Can I?"

Rose sighed. "Go ahead. I'll wait here."

She plunked down in the sand, kicked off her shoes and sunk her feet into the water lapping up on shore. She wiggled her toes and stared at the luscious blue water of Maple Bay that opened into the broad expanse of Lake Michigan.

Closing her eyes, she leaned back on her hands and tipped her face toward the sun. It was hot, but nice, especially with her feet up to her ankles in water that bordered on cold. She was glad she hadn't gone swimming. At least, that's what she wanted to believe. Where had all the fun in her life gone?

She suddenly felt drops of water and sat up quick.

"You should come in. The water's great." Cam shook his head, sending more droplets raining over her as he slipped back into his T-shirt.

"It's too cold." Rose wiped off the water from her skin before zeroing in on her son. He was jumping off the raft with a couple of boys from the group.

"Some things never change." Cam nodded toward where kids jumped and dove into the water only to climb back out and do it again. And again.

Rose wasn't so sure about that but watched the activity viewed by a male lifeguard perched in a tall white chair with red lifesaving rings looped on either side. The kid had a smear of zinc on his nose and didn't look that much older than those he watched.

"Can you swim?"

Rose glared at him. "Of course I can, but that doesn't mean I want to wearing jeans."

"It'll loosen you up." He grinned at her, completely unrepentant for tossing out such a passive insult.

"I think I'll stay tight and dry." Loosening up led to trouble.

"This feels like the summers I remember." Cam grinned as he sat next to her, looking out over the water. "My brothers and I used to come here after school and swim as early as mid-May. It was a game to see who'd go in first."

"You must have a lot of memories here."

He nodded. "Both good and not so good. We're the reason there's a lifeguard on that raft. My brother Darren started a fight with a couple of the Bay Willows kids that ended in an all-out brawl when I was about Greg's age."

Rose's eyes widened. "Did you get into trouble?"

Cam shrugged. "My dad gave us a good talking-to, but we weren't grounded or anything. It was just kid stuff. Locals versus Bay Willows."

Rose looked at him. "Bay Willows?"

"A wealthy lakeside summer community right over there." He pointed in the distance toward huge sweeping willow trees that banked the shoreline.

"The road with the huge old houses?"

Cam nodded. "The same."

"Maybe it's not so different up here." Rose stared at her son on the raft, her brow marred by worry. "I sure don't want Greg getting into fights."

"It's what boys do." Cam shrugged.

He didn't understand that fights were a big deal and could get worse. They had definitely been taken seriously at Greg's old school. "Not at all what I want to hear."

"There's probably not a mom out there who wants their boy getting into a fight."

"Or more fights. Greg had some trouble last year with fighting at school."

"Do you know what they were about?"

"Name-calling mostly." Rose had been shocked at how mean kids could be when she'd been called by the principal.

"Sometimes you can ignore insults for only so long." Cam looked as if he'd been there and done that.

"That doesn't make it right. And it's certainly no example of turning the other cheek."

Cam chuckled. "Fights happen."

Rose felt her eyes widen. "Please don't tell me you're still getting into fights…"

He raised his hands in surrender. "No, no. Not since I was a kid. Still, you can't keep the boy in a bubble."

"And you know about raising kids, how?" Rose stood and waved Greg in. It was time to go.

Cam shook his head. "I don't, but I do have younger brothers and sisters I had to watch over sometimes. I'm one of ten kids."

Rose did a double take. "Wow."

"Yeah, wow. Look, I'm sorry if I'm sticking my nose where it doesn't belong, but I'm trying to help."

"Because of your deal with God."

He smiled. "Something like that, sure."

Rose appreciated the sentiment, but she wasn't sure she trusted it, or him. "So, tell me what you meant about filling in as a cook next week."

"I have an idea. I might be able to talk my mom into filling in this weekend while I'm gone. She's good, Rose, and I think she can handle it."

Rose felt her jaw drop. "Seriously?"

"Come on, we can talk about it walking back to the diner. Then, if you find someone you'd like to hire, I can help transition them next week after I get back from my tournament."

She nodded, unsure how to take this man and his help.

After they'd returned to the diner in order to review those financials a little more, Cam kicked himself for showing his hand too soon. He hadn't asked his mom to fill in while he chased his last chance to qualify for next year's fishing series. He'd have some more time to fill in as cook after that until the next Northern Open qualifier in August.

"Mom?" Greg's voice called from the kitchen.

"Yeah?" Rose answered.

The boy stopped at the fridge, opened it and searched the insides until finally closing the door. He scanned the counter, looked over the bakery muffins trapped in an acrylic case and kept walking toward them. "Is there anything to eat?"

"I can make you a sandwich," Rose offered.

"Nah." The kid grimaced. "Had one for lunch."

"Soup or mac and cheese."

Greg kicked at the leg of the table where they sat. "Don't we have anything else?"

"Cereal."

Greg slumped into a chair. "What are you doing?"

"Going over paperwork. Grab a snack upstairs and then we'll figure out dinner."

"There isn't anything upstairs, I already looked." Greg had already changed his clothes.

"Greg…" Rose had that mom tone in her voice, as if now wasn't the time to discuss their lack of foodstuff. Her cheeks flushed a pretty color.

Cam checked his watch. It was after five. "Why don't you guys come to my place for dinner?"

Rose looked like a deer caught in headlights.

"Can we, Mom?"

"I don't know." Rose stood, looking flustered.

"Please?" the boy begged.

It was only dinner, with her son in tow. Even if Cam wanted to, he wouldn't make any moves on

Rose with her son around. "I have a couple steaks that need grilling. You'd be doing me a favor."

"Yes, but—" She glanced at Greg's hope-filled face.

He could see her resolve weaken and went ahead and sealed the deal. "We can finish up the returns afterward and get it done, so you'll know now instead of later."

He knew time was ticking for her to make a decision on the Deans' offer. He also knew better than to give his opinion regarding what he thought she should do. He didn't want the responsibility that came with all that. He'd blown up his own life; no sense blowing up hers.

"Okay." She looked down at her jeans and T-shirt. "Maybe I should change."

Cam waved that idea away. "You're fine. Let's go."

"All right!" Greg dashed for the kitchen and the alley entrance.

Rose gathered up the financial paperwork. "Let me grab my purse. It's upstairs. I'll be right back."

Cam nodded and followed Greg. "We'll be here."

Rose tore up the steps.

He turned to her son. "So, how was your first day at summer youth group?"

Greg made a face. "We played golf."

"Not a golfer, I take it?" Cam had never liked the game, either. Seemed like a waste of time.

"It's so boring. We walked forever and had to whisper and not goof around."

Cam chuckled. "So, I take it that you went around here."

Greg nodded. "Yup. Nine holes. I think it was called Bay Willows."

"That's a nice place." Although the Bay Willows golf club was open to the public, the course rules were strict and stuffy. Play time must have been donated by a church member, since John couldn't afford to pay for all of the group to go.

The kid groaned. "It was awful. Until we went to the beach."

Cam laughed.

"What was awful?"

"Playing golf," Greg said.

Cam looked up as Rose came down the steps. Her *purse* was big enough to hold those tax returns plus a host of other things. More like a soft briefcase and certainly not the dainty things his sisters carried. Rose hadn't changed her clothes, but when she reached the bottom step, that delicate fragrance wafted around him. She'd put on more of that delicious perfume.

For him?

Nope, couldn't be. Women did that sort of thing. Monica used to douse herself every time she left the house. Still, what if Rose made a move on him? His skin tingled at the thought no matter how laughable.

Rose's gaze challenged him to move out of her way. "Ready?"

Cam backed up and held open the door. One whiff of her appealing cologne had him rethinking his offer. Maybe dinner at his place wasn't such a good idea. "After you."

Rose gave him a curious look. "So, how far of a walk is it?"

"Ugh! Are we walking?" Greg's voice cracked.

He laughed. "Sorry, bud, more walking. It's not far, maybe three blocks."

Rose looked at her son, alarmed. "What's the matter with walking?"

"He did nine holes of golf today."

"Greg…" Rose gave her son the classic get-over-it mom smirk.

Cam had seen that same look often enough from his own mom. Expressions like that must come with the territory of raising kids. He liked kids, but had never thought he'd ever raise any of his own.

Greg responded in kind. "What? I'm tired."

"And hungry," Cam added with a wink.

"Yeah. And hungry, too."

Rose elbowed him, but smiled. "Don't encourage him."

Cam smiled back. He liked this teasing side of Rose. Maybe too much.

Rose listened to her son's chatter, but he wasn't talking to her. He was telling Cam all about his day at group. They'd always been a team, but he'd been pulling away this last year. Probably natural for a kid his age.

Seeing her son excited was indeed a victory. Greg had sulked ever since they'd moved in. He didn't do much but play video games and watch TV when he wasn't helping her in the diner. She'd split her tips with him and Greg liked the money but he needed fun and the summer program had worked.

Rose whispered a prayer of gratitude once again. God had provided this opportunity to move Greg into a smaller school system before he hit high school. It was something she'd fretted about for a while and then Linda had left them her diner and Rose's parents had agreed moving to Maple Springs was a good decision. She'd learned that God heard her prayers. Looking back, He'd answered so many.

A pair of bright blue eyes slashed through her mind, but she refused to consider Cam as anyone other than a Good Samaritan filling in as her cook in a pinch. Watching the genuine interest he gave her son warmed her heart, but a man like Cam could *not* be an answer to prayer.

And we know that all things work together for good to them that love God, to them who are the called according to His purpose.

This morning's devotional verse from Romans came to mind. It reaffirmed that God had her back. It reaffirmed that she needed to quit worrying about everything and pray more. No, trust more. Rose prayed all the time, like a broken record she hoped God wouldn't tire of hearing.

As they strolled away from downtown Maple Springs, the coil of tension she'd tried to let go of grew tighter. She looked around at all the pretty houses, the big houses, and wondered if she'd ever afford one of her own.

Finally, Cam opened the gate of a white picket fence. "Here we are."

It was modest as far as homes went in the area, but still beautiful. A turn-of-the-century two-story white clapboard-sided house with black shutters sat in an oversize village lot with overgrown pink roses spilling over the fence. "Wow. This is where you live?"

"I bought it several years ago."

Rose couldn't keep the surprise out of her voice. "You bought it? But it's big, like for a family."

"It's not that big, not compared to some. I got a great deal after the mortgage crisis rippled its way up here. It was too good an investment to pass up. I used to share it with my brother Matthew, but now that he's married, it's just me."

"Mom, come here. Look at his boat!" Greg hollered from the driveway.

Rose trotted after her son.

"Isn't this cool?" Greg ran his fingers along the side of a dark red boat with black slashes.

"That's some paint job." Rose scanned the area that was Cam's home. The placement of the two-car garage with a high-peaked roof sporting a window on the second floor created privacy in the backyard where a deck had been built off the back of the house.

It was a beautiful property, a dreamy kind of place, and yet Cam had purchased it merely as an investment. This house wasn't his home, but a future bank account. Another indication that Cam had no intention of settling down or sticking around.

He tapped the dark gray carpeted platform in the front of the boat. "Color's called dark cherry. I had it repainted after removing sponsor stickers."

So this was a professional fishing boat. It looked shiny and fast and the sides seemed awfully low to her. It'd be so easy to fall overboard. Toward the back were two deep seats, one behind a console with a steering wheel. Then a smaller platform stretched the back of the boat. A huge motor perched between two black poles finished off the end.

"What are those?" Rose pointed at the poles.

"Shallow water anchors. They're hydraulic and pretty cool."

"Wow." Greg ran his hands up and down the metal. "How do they work?"

"Don't touch, okay? We don't want to break anything." Rose might not know much when it came to fishing, but she knew expensive. Cam's boat had to have cost a pretty penny.

"He's fine. This thing's tough as nails." Cam turned to her son. "At the flip of a switch, these poles fold down into the water and act as anchors in depths up to eight feet. It's great when I want to fish the shallows and not drift. Keeps the boat in place and stable."

Greg's eyes grew wide with wonder. "Where do you keep the fish?"

Cam climbed up into the boat using the trailer's wheel well, then reached down for Greg. "Come up and I'll show you."

Before Rose could refuse, her son was in the boat with a king-of-the-hill look on his face. She shook her head when Cam offered her his hand. "No thank you, I'll watch from here."

Cam opened various storage compartments that were in the platform floor. Places for gear and a live well to keep the fish fresh. A third seat also popped up between the two. He clearly took pride in showcasing this boat, even to an eleven-year-old boy soon to be twelve.

Cam looked at her. "I'm going fishing tomorrow after work with my cousin Tommy. There's room for Greg to go."

"Mom, can I?" Greg's excitement was palpable.

Rose could have clocked Cam for asking in front of her son. He knew she'd have a hard time refusing, but refuse she must. What if Greg fell over that low edge? "I don't know."

"Awww, come on, Mom…"

"Greg!" Rose snapped. "Let me think on it."

Cam jumped out of the boat onto the pavement in front of her. "He'll be perfectly safe wearing a life jacket."

She glared at him. He didn't play fair. "I said, I'll think about it."

Unrepentant, Cam grinned at her. "Don't take too long."

"Yeah, Mom." Greg jumped down like Cam and the two headed for the house, talking fish and boat speeds. "Don't take too long."

Rose gritted her teeth and followed them inside.

Entering the house from the driveway, Rose walked into a mudroom that served as a laundry area. The interior was clean and tidy even with Cam's jackets hanging on hooks and his boots lined up against one wall. A basket of folded clothes sat atop the dryer bathed in sunlight from an open window.

A galley-style kitchen came next with a cozy family room and eating area complete with a fireplace to the right. Windows ran along the far wall overlooking the backyard. The rest of the house lay to the left.

"Make yourselves at home and I'll get the grill started." Cam flashed her another one of his killer smiles and disappeared through a sliding glass door onto the back deck.

Rose didn't need further prodding to check this place out. She headed left and scouted the rest of the downstairs. Cam's home was simply furnished but clean. Window blinds replaced curtains and the walls had been painted a warm cream. So much potential here, and yet it was sort of sterile. The sign of a man who wasn't home much.

"Mom, come here and look at this."

Rose turned but didn't see her son. "Where are you?"

"In here." He stuck his head out of a side room.

"Don't snoop." Rose was drawn to whatever her son had found and entered the small den complete with a desk and computer and overstuffed love seat.

Her mouth dropped open when she spotted the trophies covering one wall. Big ones, little ones and plaques. Even a framed check stub. She stepped in for closer inspection— *Whoa.* The amount was a cool twenty-five thousand dollars. All of the bling belonged to Cam from various fishing tournaments all over the Midwest, Northeast and down South. They spanned several years, too. He hadn't been kidding about the professional part. This little man cave showcased serious accomplishment.

"Ah, you found the trophy room."

Rose jumped at the sound of Cam's voice. "Pretty impressive."

"You won all these?" Greg looked truly in awe of the man who had been known before only as the cool guy who made the best cheeseburgers.

Cam nodded. "You're looking at over twenty years of competitive fishing. As many tournaments where I've placed well or won, there's probably five times that where I didn't."

"How old were you when you started?" Rose asked.

"I was Greg's age when I joined a local bass fishing club. Fishing kept me out of trouble for the most part." Cam gently picked up a small plaque, running his finger over the brass plate bearing his name. "And thirteen when I won my first tournament."

Rose read the longing in Cam's eyes as he stared at that trophy, apparently lost in a fond memory.

Then that blue gaze hardened with determination. He clearly wanted back out there. Bad.

"What about this one?" Greg pointed at a square trophy with a fish on top.

Cam chuckled, but his eyes glittered with something dark. Bad memory, or was that regret? "My first pro tournament win for a cash prize. The check on the wall."

Greg spotted photo albums and reached for them. "Can I look at these?"

"Knock yourself out." Cam pulled a few and handed them over to Greg.

Her son settled onto the love seat and thumbed through photos of Cam and other professional fishermen at tournaments. Everyone was dressed in gear splattered with brand names and advertisers. *Sponsors.*

The pressure of making a living at this had to be great and costly if the boat outside was any indication. Maybe that's where sponsors came in, but he'd lost his.

"Is it common to lose sponsors?" The question fell out of her mouth before she realized how intrusive it sounded. "I'm sorry."

"No, it's fine." Cam ran a hand through his already messy hair. "And yes, especially after low placements a few seasons in row. Some guys have the same sponsors for years, others switch up and garner more as they succeed in climbing to the top. I won a tournament a couple years ago and that boat out there was the prize."

"Wow. Have you ever thought about doing something else?" Rose scanned the shelves of trophies. Was there anything he'd like better than the thrill of this kind of competition? Surely the stress was high with the pressure to perform well.

"No." Cam chuckled, but it sounded more bitter than amused. "Not much else I'm good at."

Rose stared at him. She didn't believe that for a second. "You're an excellent cook."

"Speaking of which, the grill is no doubt ready for those steaks." Cam nearly bolted for the kitchen.

Rose followed. "I can make a salad if you have the fixings."

"I do." Cam pulled out a drawer. "Knives are in here and cutting boards and big bowls in the cupboard below."

"Okay." Rose waited while Cam washed his hands at the sink, then called to her son while she did the same. "Greg, why don't you bring those albums out here?"

"Awww, Mom."

Cam glanced at her before heading outside with a platter of steaks and seasonings. "He's fine in there till dinner. There's nothing he can get into that he shouldn't see."

Rose nodded, but she looked in on Greg anyway. "Don't touch anything but those photo albums, understand?"

Her son nodded but didn't even look up from one of three albums on his lap.

Rose snuck a peek at the pages Greg had opened. Cam stood on a dock with his arm around another man and both were holding fish. Cam looked glorious with a wide smile and tousled hair gleaming in the sun. She'd love it if Cam stayed on as her cook, but really, what could she offer that beat what radiated from that picture?

Cam's words echoed through her thoughts. *Not much else I'm good at.*

Greg looked up at her. "Can I please go fishing with Cam?"

Every boy deserves to fish. More of Cam's words.

She looked at Greg. Her father had warned about smothering her son. He needed to stretch his wings. Someone once said where there's little risk, there's little gain, and Rose had played it safe for so long because of losing instead of gaining. She sighed. "Okay. You can go, but promise me you'll wear a life jacket the whole time."

He beamed at her and nodded. "Thanks, Mom. You're the best."

Her heart swelled to bursting. She leaned down and kissed the top of his head. "You are, too."

He shrugged away and grabbed another photo album. "This is so cool."

"Yup. Pretty cool." Rose made her way back to the kitchen at the same time Cam returned from the back deck. Their gazes locked and held.

Rose felt like she'd jumped into the deep end. "I told Greg he can go with you tomorrow."

Cam smiled. "Good call."

She hoped so. She hoped she'd made the right decision.

Chapter Five

❧

Cam scrubbed four big potatoes with a vengeance while Rose sliced tomatoes for the salad next to him. It didn't matter where he stood or where she stood in this galley kitchen—she was much too close. Her presence filled the space right along with the delicious scent of her perfume.

Having Rose in his kitchen felt right somehow and that scared him. He didn't have women over to cook.

While he'd chopped shallots and fresh tarragon, he'd noticed the slow, methodical way she sliced a tomato. She'd cut cucumbers the same way, as if she wasn't used to doing this very often. "How can you be in the restaurant business and not know how to cook?"

Her cheeks flushed and she paused mid-slice. "As a kid, I had no interest in learning, so my mom didn't teach me. In college I ate on campus or while on duty at the restaurant where I wait-ressed in the evenings."

"Did Kurt cook?" If he was anything like his younger brothers, Rose was better off without him. Of course, now the guy was dead, but still.

Rose let loose a bitter snort. "He was on the road most of the time with music gigs. When he was home, we'd go out so he could be seen. After he left us, I moved back home to my mom's cook-ing."

Cam shook his head. "How'd you two meet?"

Rose dumped sliced carrots into the salad, then reached to rinse off her hands in the side of the sink he wasn't using. Reaching for the towel, her arm brushed against his, sending a jolt of aware-ness straight to his toes.

She sighed. "He and his band played a couple of venues in Kalamazoo, and they frequented the restaurant where I worked. We met, he swept me off my feet and we eloped."

Cam would never have guessed Rose Dean could do something that impulsive. "How old were you?"

"Eighteen. My parents were not happy, espe-cially when we moved to Nashville so Kurt could pursue his country music career."

"Is that where Greg was born?"

"Yup, seven months later." She lowered her voice. "He was a big surprise. A tour bus was no place for a newborn and I jumped off the party train. I think Kurt resented that along with his responsibilities. He stayed away more often than not. Then he didn't come home at all."

He could read between what she said and didn't say. The hard look in Rose's eyes pretty much confirmed a husband gone astray. Hadn't she said that Greg was only six the last time he'd seen his father? Kurt had blown off his family. His wife and young son, for what? Cam could easily guess. The guy had been a fool.

He tossed the cleaned potatoes in the microwave and hit the button for baked potatoes hard. "You didn't remarry."

"No. I dated a guy, but…" She looked away.

"But what?" Cam prodded.

She skewered him with a challenging stare, and her voice dropped again to a whisper. "Not many want a ready-made family."

Greg. Hadn't Cam thought something similar about taking on someone's kids? Yeah, because of his own failures. Not because of anything wrong with them. Greg was a good kid.

He bent down and retrieved a saucepan, threw in a glob of butter and placed it on the stove. Turning the gas knob to low, he looked at her. "Can you stir this around till it's melted? I'm going to flip the steaks."

"Hurry back." Panic raced across her face. "I mean, I don't want to burn it."

He chuckled and handed her the plate of shallots and tarragon. "Toss this in when it's all melted. I'll be right back."

Rose bit down on her lower lip and nodded, never taking her eyes off the butter in the pan.

He hesitated, watching her a moment longer.

"Go. I think I got this." Rose waved him away. She had no idea how tempting she looked.

Cam made a quick exit. He needed distance before he did something he shouldn't, like trying to sweep her off her feet. On the deck, he lifted the grill and flipped the thick steaks, turning down the flame. They'd be done soon, somewhere between medium-rare and medium. Perfect.

Back inside, Rose hadn't left her post. He watched her dump the onions and herbs into the butter. The rich aroma surrounded them and the sizzle made him think that he knew what those shallots felt like. He tossed in a small amount of vinegar followed by half a cup or so of white wine and increased the heat so it would reduce.

Rose looked up. "Smells good. What is it going to be?"

"Béarnaise sauce."

She nodded. "I've never seen it made before."

"You're the one making it, sweet cheeks." He grinned at the wide-eyed look she gave him.

"I can do without the name-calling."

He laughed outright when he realized she was teasing him right back. "Keep stirring while I get the rest of the ingredients."

Cam separated a couple eggs and beat the yolks in a small metal bowl and added heavy cream before setting it aside. He unwrapped two sticks of butter and tossed them into the pan. Once they melted, he turned off the heat completely.

"Now what?" Rose asks.

"Get ready to stir quickly while I pour this in." He handed over a wire whisk and then drizzled in the yolk mix, but Rose wasn't whisking fast enough.

"No, no, like this." With one hand around her back, he drizzled in the yolks, then placing his other hand over hers, he increased the pressure and speed of whisking. "It's all in the wrist."

She had little room to move and actually leaned into his chest as she sloughed off his hand, whisking furiously. "Like this?"

This close, he couldn't help it. He inhaled near her neck, practically touching his nose to her skin. "Man, you smell good."

The whisk flipped out of Rose's hand, splattering butter sauce in every direction before hitting the floor. She jumped aside, knocking the metal bowl out of his hand into the pan of béarnaise sauce.

Cam thought it funny until he saw the dismay in her eyes. He immediately backed up and raised his hands in surrender. "Rose, I'm sorry."

Those sweet cheeks of hers blazed red-hot. She uttered an awkward chuckle, picked up the whisk and rinsed it off. "No, I'm sorry. I haven't, I mean, it's been a while and, well, you're an attractive man."

Cam was glad she didn't look at him. It gave him time to control the desire to wrap his arms around her. Slipping into his safety zone, Cam flirted instead. "So, you think I'm easy on the eyes, huh?"

Rose laughed, tension eased. "I said attractive."

He winked. "I know what you meant."

She shook her head. "Shouldn't you check the steaks?"

"Yeah, and you can get that bowl out of our béarnaise sauce and whisk it while I'm gone."

"Aye, aye, Chef."

Cam exited through the open slider. He'd never thought himself a chef before. He cooked. Lifting the grill lid, he decided the steaks looked a little overdone, more toward medium.

He blew out his breath as he switched off the gas. He felt a little singed around the edges, too. No matter how attracted he might be to Rose, she wasn't a woman to be kissed and discarded.

Cam didn't want to be another one of those men in her life.

Besides, there was Greg to consider. He deserved a stand-up father figure. Cam wasn't ready for marriage and a family. He had few skills outside of fishing and that career had been tainted by cheating. These were certainly not the actions he'd want a kid he cared about to imitate or even know about.

He'd teach Greg how to fish. It had kept him out of trouble as a teen, so he'd return the favor. He'd do his best to help Rose keep her diner, too, and then be on his way. Cam had nothing to offer until he redeemed not only his fishing career but his name and self-respect.

After a dinner filled with talk of the upcoming fishing trip, Rose and Greg loaded the dishwasher while Cam put away leftovers. There wasn't much, only some salad and an extra potato. Rose had never been so thankful for Greg's presence at dinner. Her son had carried the mealtime conversation. Cam was good with Greg, answering his barrage of questions about fishing and even asking a few questions, too, gauging Greg's patience level for sitting in a boat.

The whole time, Rose had been all too aware of Cam. Too easily she recalled the warmth of him standing behind her with his hand guiding hers in making that butter sauce. She'd let him get too close. She'd wanted to ignore that with Cam came all that risky baggage she'd rather not unpack.

"Ready to finish up those tax returns?" Cam stood near the counter, looking completely at ease. "I can make us some coffee."

"Yes, please." Rose wiped down the table. Reality had a way of crashing in. She couldn't escape yet. Those financials were the reason she was here, along with a home-cooked meal for Greg.

"You got it." He ground whole beans and filled the coffeemaker.

"Hey, Cam," Greg asked. "Can I watch TV?"

"Yep. The remote's on the stand."

"Not too loud." Rose needed to concentrate without a TV blaring in the background.

"We can go into the living room," Cam offered.

"This table is fine. More room to spread out." Rose wasn't about to get cozy on the couch. Staying in the same room with Greg only a few feet away was much safer.

The scent of fresh coffee teased her nose as she pulled the paperwork package out of her purse along with a notepad where she'd jotted down some of Cam's tips on reading returns. Scanning those notes, she looked over the most recent year, but the papers still looked like a mash of numbers with little meaning.

"Here." Cam set a mug of steaming coffee before her.

"Thank you." She took a sip and smiled. "Perfect."

"You drink yours like I do." He smiled back.

Rose got lost in his eyes. Something sweet and caring shone there that tugged at her resolve to keep her distance. Maybe the flirting was better. She could ignore that, but this warm concern, as if he really cared, was far too tempting. It had been so long since she'd been held, and Cam had strong arms.

He sat down and pulled the paperwork closer. "Okay, where'd we leave off?"

"Something about deductions."

"Right. Think of them as business expenses. The cost of doing business. So gross receipts minus those deductions are your profits. And what you're taxed on."

Rose scooted closer and pointed at the first page. "So, what's depreciation?"

"It's the ability to write off an asset's decrease in value as an expense. Everything loses value over time compared to what you originally paid for it."

Rose looked at him, finally understanding. "Ahh, I see."

"What was your major in college?"

She laughed. "It was going to be Business."

"They didn't go over any of this?" Cam chuckled, too.

"I don't know. My first semester I had signed up for only general stuff and then I dropped out." She scanned the couch where Greg had slumped over, fast asleep. "After he was born, there never seemed to be the time nor money to go back. What about you?"

"Didn't go."

That surprised her. "Seriously?"

He looked at her hard as if searching for the right words. "When I said that fishing is the only thing I'm good at, I meant it. I'm not much of a reader, so college wasn't an option. Not in my mind anyway. I pursued professional bass fishing."

It registered that she hadn't seen any books around his house, not even recipe books in the kitchen. Only photo albums were shelved in his study and a few fishing magazines graced the man's coffee table near where Greg snoozed.

Greg had been diagnosed with a mild case of dyslexia in third grade. If she hadn't gone through that experience with him, she might have let Cam's comment go. That distinct lack of reading material pushed her to prod. "You don't like to read or is it hard to read?"

A flash of shame in his eyes was quickly doused and he looked away, clearly uncomfortable.

Her heart twisted. She was certainly no expert, but she'd coached Greg through several exercises they'd learned at a special class. Maybe she could help, but she'd need to know what she was up against. "Cam, what happens when you read?"

He looked confused. "What do you mean?"

"I want to help. Especially since you've helped me with so much." She lifted the returns to drive home her point.

He laughed then, a quick sound more like a sarcastic bark than amusement. "I'm not illiterate, if that's what you're getting at. I get by."

She had no doubt he got by, but how? His joking hid vulnerability underneath, as well as deflection. He didn't want to talk about this. How bad was it? "Were you ever tested in school?"

Cam didn't meet her gaze. "I suppose. I was in the slow readers group."

"If you're willing to give it a try, I can help."

He looked at her, really looked at her, and then it was as if a curtain had been drawn across his brilliant blue eyes, blocking her view. Then he grinned at her—wide and teasing. The flirt was back in full force. "You'd be my private tutor?"

"I'm serious."

He wiggled his eyebrows at her. "Me, too."

But he wasn't. Not at all. She could see how it would be—he'd sit too close and tease like he was now and make her uncomfortable. More deflection. They wouldn't get anywhere reading-wise.

"Right." Hadn't she thought that his flirting was preferable to genuine concern? Not this time. Not when he used it to shut her out.

Cam looked down at the scattered tax returns. "Shall we finish up?"

"Yes." She nodded toward the couch. "I'd better get Greg home."

As Cam recapped what they'd gone over, Rose watched him closely. He hid behind that charm, masking the real man under those good-time smiles. She liked glimpses of the hidden Cam, the real Cam, a lot more.

What would happen if she turned the tables on him, gave him some of his own treatment? She really should help him, for all he'd done for her. Taking a deep breath, she laid her hand on his arm. His skin felt warm and strong, but tense, like a string pulled too tight.

His gaze flew to hers.

Rose smiled at the panic in his eyes and forced her hand to remain still. "If you'd like to work on reading together, let me know. Greg has issues, too, so I've learned some methods that may help."

He stared a moment longer.

Rose didn't look away. She couldn't read his expression, either.

Giving her a slow smile, Cam covered her hand with his own. "You're the only one I'd call."

Her breath caught. Okay, so her plan backfired, but in this heart-pounding game of chicken she wouldn't flinch first.

Maybe she was the one with the disorder, attracted to yet another wrong man. Cam was definitely wrong for her. A man after the thrill of competition and prize money, he'd never stay home. A man who preferred flirting to being real with a woman—would he stay true?

Bested, Rose blew out her breath and stood, gathering up her paperwork. "I've got to go."

Cam stood, too. "I can drive you home."

Shaking her son's shoulder to wake him, she glanced outside. The sun had set but it wasn't yet dark. "Thanks, but I'd rather walk. Thank you for dinner."

"You're welcome." He accepted her refusal of a ride without teasing her further and walked them to the door. "See you tomorrow."

"Bright and early." Rose led a sleepy Greg outside, but glanced back and waved good-night. She caught a look of such defeat on Cam's face that it sliced through her, sharp and painful.

He hadn't seen her, but she'd seen him with startling clarity. The real Cam was a hurting man. Rose couldn't deny the strong urge to help him as he'd helped her, but by doing so, she'd expose herself to a world of hurt if she let this attraction grow into something she couldn't handle.

Whispering under her breath, she prayed for God's guidance and then she prayed for Cam. He'd admitted to trying to be a better person. What other regrets lurked beneath that charming facade he showed the world, and did she dare find out?

The following day at the diner, Cam kept his distance from Rose as best he could. It wasn't too hard since they'd been busy from the moment they opened up the doors. Still, the woman was scary. He'd never admitted his reading issues to anyone, yet he'd told Rose.

He'd never been comfortable with his failings, but admitting his trouble with reading hadn't bothered Rose. She hadn't viewed him as some idiot. Quite the opposite, in fact. If he was smart, he'd forget the softness that had crept into her eyes when she'd figured him out. He'd forget her offer, too.

He didn't for a minute doubt that her offer to help him read had been heartfelt and genuine. Accepting would only lead to more admissions of how low he'd sunk to get by. Cam didn't want to lose Rose's good opinion. Not by a long shot.

It had taken every ounce of his willpower to switch gears once she'd laid down her challenge along with the burning touch of her hand. He'd fought fire with fire, yet he'd been the one burned. Consumed with desire to be more than he was. A man he could never be—

"Hey, Cam, you look like you know what you're doing."

A familiar voice scattered his thoughts. Cam grinned at his cousin Tommy. "Of course I know what I'm doing. You here for lunch?"

"Got out of work early, so you can pick me up at home later. Got any walleye back there?" Tommy nodded toward the kitchen.

Cam chuckled and handed him a plastic-covered menu. "Nope, but the special is a tuna melt with onion rings."

"Sounds pretty good. But really, what are you doing working here?"

At that moment Rose breezed over to put in an order, so Cam cupped her elbow to keep her from darting off to the next table. "Rose, this is my cousin Tommy. He's going fishing with me and Greg."

"Nice to meet you." She extended her hand. "Make sure he gets home safe and sound."

Tommy returned the handshake. "We'll take good care of your boy. Cam said this is the first time he's gone. If anyone can teach a kid to fish, it's me."

Rose glanced at Cam and then burst out laughing. "Ah, now I see the family resemblance. Cam said the same thing."

"Just speaking truth." Cam grinned.

"I appreciate that." Rose had a teasing glint in her eye. "Got to run, looks like someone wants their check."

After she'd gone, Tommy gave him an all-knowing nod. "Now I get it."

"Get what?" Cam scanned the new order for two more specials and a chef's salad.

"You work for one pretty lady."

Cam glanced at Rose settling a bill at the cash register. Her smile lit up her face. She had a lovely face, beautiful even. Looking closer, he detected a hint of makeup today. Not a lot, but a smudge of smoky color defined her pretty green eyes. The light green top she wore was more feminine than those baggy T-shirts she usually wore. This one showed off her trim waist and the slight flare of her hips—

He frowned. What was up with that?

"Well, slide me under a nickel."

"What?" Cam got busy making those two specials.

"You're sweet on her."

"You going to order or what?"

Tommy laughed. "Yeah, give me the tuna. You make that plate look awfully pretty, dude."

"Thanks." Cam spotted Greg filling water

glasses and waved the boy over. He'd skipped group today, so he could go fishing right after close.

Let Tommy see what came with being *sweet on Rose*. If anyone knew Cam wasn't ready for a family, it was his cousin. They'd fished together since they were kids. Tommy had even joined Cam in a few tournaments as his co-angler. The guy was happily married and wedged in tight here in Maple Springs with his own business to run, so he couldn't get away often. Tommy knew how hard it was for Cam to have a serious relationship, because there hadn't been any.

Jess, the new waitress, also put in an order. "Two more specials."

Cam nodded. He introduced Greg to Tommy and wasn't surprised when the boy slid into the next seat.

"We're taking your boat, right, Cam?"

Cam nodded as he constructed two more tuna melts.

"He's got a pretty sweet boat, don't he?" Tommy sipped the diet cola Cam had served him.

Cam smiled. He'd fished well at a regional tournament where he'd won it. He'd fished clean because he'd had a different observer in the boat each day instead of a co-angler. Polygraphs on big wins were commonplace and although Cam had beat them before, he didn't take chances if he didn't have to.

"Coolest one I've ever seen. So, what kind of fish are we after?" Greg tried to sound like he knew what he was doing.

"I tell you right now, kid, the only fish worth fishing for is walleye."

Greg's gaze flew to Cam's. "What about bass?"

"All fine and good if you're after some trophy, but if you want to eat well, you want walleye."

Cam chuckled. "Pike are good, and fun to catch."

Tommy snorted. "Aw, come on, man, pike will hit anything. No skill there."

And so the conversation continued. Cam filled orders while chatting with his cousin and a couple other guys seated at the counter about where the best fish were biting and which lures to use.

Greg soaked it in with wide-eyed wonder until Rose tapped him on the shoulder. "Hey, Mom, this is Tommy."

"We've met." Rose smiled. "I need you to bus some tables while Chris is washing dishes in back."

Greg's shoulders drooped, but he didn't complain. He got up and did his mom's bidding.

"Good kid," Tommy said.

"He's a great kid," Cam said.

Greg had been a big help this morning. Cam

made a mental note to check with Rose if anyone had applied for the cook position today. He glanced at Greg as the kid cleared a table. Cam looked forward to showing the boy how to fish. He looked forward to fishing for the fun of it and today promised a good time of relaxation.

It had been a couple days since Cam had been out on the lakes, putting in practice time. He needed to get out there more, though. Fishing wasn't only something he enjoyed, it was work. *His* work, and he looked forward to returning to it this weekend with good results. He had to fish well.

Chapter Six

~⟋~

After closing the diner, Cam and Greg hurried with cleanup along with the busboy. Jess demonstrated a heart of gold by helping out, too, so they could get out of there quickly. By 2:20, everything was done. Cam was ready to go and Rose was…where?

He looked around but didn't see her, so he nodded to Greg. "You might want to grab a sweatshirt. It can get cool later on the water."

"Be right back." Greg ran toward the stairs, only to be met by Rose holding out that very thing to her son.

"I'm heading over to Linda's attorney's office in case you get back before me." She'd slipped on a tan-colored blazer over her green top and jeans. Her lips were slicked with a rosy-colored gloss.

He wouldn't mind finding out if it was flavored. Shaking off that thought, he realized her extra care with her appearance today made sense. No doubt, Rose wanted to make a good impression on the attorney. This pretty new look had nothing to do with him.

"We'll be home much later than that. I'll have my cell and you've got the number."

"Yes, and here's mine." Rose tapped her phone, making his buzz.

He added her personal number to his contacts, right above the diner. "Got it. Any bites on the ad for a cook?"

"No." Rose pursed her lips, catching his focus yet again.

"My mother agreed to fill in this weekend, by the way."

Rose stared at him, slack-jawed. "Really? Wow."

"Her parents managed a golf club once upon a time, so she grew up helping out in the kitchen."

"Thank you."

"No problem." Cam shrugged. "She'll work with me tomorrow, then take over Thursday through Saturday. I'll be back Monday. And you're not to pay her—I've got this. Okay?"

"Okay." Rose squared her shoulders as she turned to her son. "Be careful, Greg. Listen to Cam and Tommy. And wear—"

"I know, a life jacket." Greg finished her sentence.

"Have fun." Rose leaned toward her son, but he

pulled back. She bit her bottom lip and glanced at him with worry and motherly concern all wrapped into one helpless look. "So, he doesn't need a license?"

Cam stepped close enough to catch a hint of her perfume. It was the same sweet and flowery scent. "No. He's under seventeen. Don't worry, he'll be fine. I promise."

"I'm holding you to that." Her voice might be soft but the intensity of it came across loud and clear.

"Awww, Mom." Greg rolled his eyes.

Cam smiled, but didn't discount Rose's feelings. She'd entrusted Greg to his care and that was huge. He wasn't going to let her down. "We'll see you later."

They left the diner and walked the three blocks to his house, where his boat was packed with gear, hitched to his truck and ready to roll. Greg seemed antsy walking beside him with his hands in his pockets and sweatshirt draped over one arm.

"Looking forward to fishing?" Cam asked.

"Yeah." The kid kicked at a small stick lying on the sidewalk. He didn't seem too excited now. Did he regret going?

"Something else on your mind?"

Greg shrugged.

Something definitely troubled the boy. "You want to talk about it?"

"Do you like my mom?"

Okay, that question threw Cam for a loop. What was the kid getting at? "Yeah, sure. She's great."

Greg didn't look satisfied. "If you asked her out, I wouldn't mind."

Cam's world shifted to a strange angle. Maybe the pull Rose had on him was too obvious. Even so, if Greg wanted to play matchmaker, fine, but Cam wasn't taking the bait. Not when he wasn't sure about far too many things. "We work together, bud."

"So?"

Cam wiped his brow. "So, we're just going to be friends, okay?"

"Oh. Okay." Greg's shoulders drooped.

He had to give the kid credit for guts and Cam was more than flattered that he'd think of him for his mom, but a change of subject was definitely needed. Fast. "Let me share a secret about fishing."

Greg grew hopeful. "Yeah?"

"The beauty of fishing is that it takes away all the worries you have. Time ceases to exist and outside life fades away. It's just you trying to catch a fish. Your biggest concern becomes what lure to try next."

His eyes widened. "Really?"

"Really." They'd arrived at his house, so he

lightly squeezed the kid's shoulder. "Let's go get Tommy and you'll see what I mean."

Greg nodded and climbed into the back seat of his truck.

Subject changed and successfully diverted.

It's been a while.

Rose's voice slipped through his thoughts, keeping the subject front and center in Cam's mind. He rubbed the back of his neck and climbed behind the wheel. He needed to be careful, really careful.

Within minutes, Cam pulled up to his cousin's driveway, where Tommy stood waiting, tackle box in one hand and a small cooler in the other. All thoughts of dating Rose dissipated like morning mist burned off by the sun.

Cam gestured toward the back. "I've got pop and water in the boat."

Tommy grinned. "I know it. These are snacks, man. The wife set us up with salami and cheese and homemade cookies."

"Get in. We're burning daylight." Cam shifted back into Drive as soon as Tommy was in the front seat.

"Where to, Mullet or Pickerel Lake?" Tommy buckled in.

"Either's fine with me."

"Which one has bigger fish?" Greg asked.

"I know a woman who pulled a six-and-a-half-pound smallmouth out of Pickerel last year." Tommy smiled.

"Can we go there?" Greg asked.

"Sure thing. There's a channel that connects it to Crooked Lake." Cam knew Tommy would shoot that suggestion down and waited for his response.

"Yeah, and you might as well kiss that pretty paint job on your propeller goodbye."

"Maybe I'm not as picky about my prop." Cam laughed when he looked at Greg through the rearview mirror. The kid's eyes were wide as saucers, so Cam explained. "A few years ago we took Tommy's boat and he got stuck in a sandbar in that channel."

"Brand-new paint job sandblasted to nothing trying to get loose. Had to dig ourselves out. I stay away from that channel."

Cam laughed again. "Don't worry, I'll keep us away from sandbars. Or we can take Pickerel to the Crooked River up to Burt Lake."

Tommy shook his head and muttered, "Some folks don't have all the fancy gear you got."

The drive wasn't far and it didn't take long to launch in Pickerel Lake. Once in the water, Cam eased the boat in reverse and turned around.

"How fast can you go?" Greg sat between him and Tom, bundled into a life jacket.

"Hang on." Cam knew this body of water well

and once they were away from shore, he opened up the throttle. The motor responded with ease. He checked the screen of his electronic fish-finder for water depths and upped the speed through the deepest section of the lake.

"Awesome." Greg fist-pumped the air.

"You're going to scare all the fish. Man, you're as bad as those WaveRunners out here." Tommy looked annoyed, and continued to grumble. "We should have taken my boat."

"And get stuck in the channel? Not a chance. The fish are pretty deep way out here and hard to scare." Cam wanted to show off his boat. Even if they didn't catch anything, the look on Greg's face made it worth gunning it. The kid loved every minute.

Finally, Cam slowed down, turned back and headed for their spot. His and Tommy's. Cutting the motor, Cam liked the slight drift they had, but he'd rely on his electronics for real success.

Stepping up to the front of the boat, he unlocked his trolling motor, tested it and then gestured for Greg to join him. "Come on up here and I'll show you what we're going to do."

"What's that?" Greg pointed at the floor.

"That's my sonar with GPS, so I can see the structure below. Really helps when trolling."

"Fancy depth reader is all it is," Tommy added.

"Let's get our gear." Opening one of his storage

compartments, Cam withdrew two fishing poles. The lighter of the two, he handed to Greg. Then, out of another compartment, he grabbed a couple different lure boxes.

"Wow, look at all those fishing lures." Greg whistled.

"Organized by type. Crankbait, spinners, jerkbait, poppers, jigs and worms, you name it." Most of the lures he had with them were for recreation. His tournament gear was locked up in his garage at home. Tommy was the only other person with a key to his professional equipment. "First thing we're going to do is cast. One rule. Keep the lure out of the boat. Those hooks can sink into skin quick, got it?"

Greg nodded.

Cam showed the boy how to attach a lure and then gave him a demonstration on how to cast. "The movement's all in the wrist. Give it a try."

Greg hesitated a minute, then tried and failed. He looked at Cam with panic in his eyes. "Why didn't it work?"

He chuckled and took the pole. "Don't forget to open the bail here, see this tab?"

Greg nodded, looking far too serious for an eleven-year-old, and tried again. This time he cast perfectly. The lure landed with a splash a good way away.

"Nice job." Cam slapped him on the back. "You

got it. Now reel it in at a good clip. Not too fast, but not slow, either. Yup, that's it. Good job."

The boy cast again and beamed when it arced through the air to land in the water with a splash. Reeling, the kid suddenly stopped. "Something's pulling on it."

"Give it a quick jerk to set the hook as soon as you feel that tug. Could be weeds, but if there's movement, you've got a fish. Keep reeling." Cam watched closely.

He gave Greg pointers but otherwise let him do the work. And then the fish surfaced. A nice-looking bass jumped straight out of the water as smallmouths were known to do.

"Did you see that!" Greg reeled faster.

Tommy had joined them at the front of the boat and hooted and hollered. "This one's got some shoulders. Nice one, kid. Don't wrestle it too much. Let it dance and get tired."

Cam stepped back to let Tom coach the boy in landing the bass. He'd never before seen a kid so filled with wonder and joy. Cam knew that feeling well, but introducing Greg to it washed through him with a completely different level of satisfaction.

They brought the fish into the boat and Greg was right there, willing to learn how to remove the hook like Tommy showed him. Carefully, Greg lifted the smallmouth, holding it up like a pro. "Can I keep it?"

It was a good size, but nowhere near a trophy. Cam reached in his pocket for his phone. "Let's get a picture and send it to your mom. The one you keep will be much bigger and go on the wall. This one, we'll throw back. Hold it up."

Greg did as bidden and smiled wider than Cam had ever seen the kid do since meeting him.

As Cam took the picture, he was hit with an overwhelming desire to be there when Greg caught his first trophy-size bass, or any fish that would be big enough for a wall mount. He not only wanted to pay for the taxidermy but see it hung on the wall. Not any wall—Cam envisioned it hanging in his home, where they'd tell story after story of fishing together.

Like what a father might do for his son.

The comparison hit hard and deep in Cam's gut, making him squirm. Is this what fatherhood felt like? This amazing pride in watching the boy's accomplishment? He'd never thought about having kids before. The responsibility was so big… too big.

Tom helped Greg release the bass, then the kid peered over Cam's arm. "Did you send it to my mom?"

"Ah, yeah. I'll do it now." He typed a quick text, attached the picture and hit Send.

"Thanks for bringing me here." Greg looked at him as if he'd been given a bucket of gold.

"You're welcome," Cam managed around the sudden lump in his throat. He gave the kid a quick fist bump while he got control. "Now let's get more fish."

"Yeah!" Greg roared.

The worried expression he'd seen a few times on Rose's face flashed through his mind. He understood her concerns. It wouldn't be long before this kid grew into a man. This fall he'd enter the seventh grade and then in a couple more years he'd enter high school. Who'd guide him around the pitfalls that faced every boy with been-there-done-that understanding?

You could.

The thought stood out clearly in Cam's thoughts and stayed there, yet who was he to be an example for anyone? He felt a hand at his shoulder.

Tommy. "Dude—you going to fish or stand there looking lost?"

He chuckled. His cousin had stated a whole lot of truth. Had he been chasing the wrong thing? Cam was lost, but now found because God had grabbed hold of him. This didn't seem like part of the deal, but then, Cam knew God worked in mysterious ways.

"Let's fish." Cam grabbed his pole.

He glanced at Greg, who happily cast and

reeled, cast and reeled. Looking at the boy, Cam sensed that maybe real purpose might have just been revealed to him, but did he have the courage to answer that call? Courage wasn't something he had in abundance. When it came down to it, Cam considered himself a coward.

Rose stared at the picture of her son that Cam had sent, her heart full. Greg was having the time of his life if that ear-to-ear grin was any indication. And he wore a life jacket as promised.

Every boy needs to learn how to fish. Cam's words came back to her yet again.

Glancing at the clock on the wall, she groaned. Nine thirty was a little late. They'd been gone for over six hours. Cam had texted that they were going to grab a bite to eat after fishing, so where were they?

She ran her fingertip over Cam's name on her cell phone, ready to call when she heard a familiar boyish laugh. Her relief was short-lived after hearing Cam's deeper, manly laugh float up from the street below. She bolted off the couch. Surely, he wasn't coming up, too? The screens in the tall windows allowed her only so much of a view directly below and she couldn't see either one of them.

Pacing the living room floor, Rose heard footsteps on the stairs and more male banter. Cam was indeed coming up with Greg. She scanned her apartment. Nothing much she could do about it. The kitchenette was tidy and overall the place was clean, but unpacked boxes stood stacked in the corner. This wasn't a nice house like Cam's, but an apartment. At least her bedding remained stashed in the large ottoman in front of the couch where she placed it every morning. Thankfully, she hadn't changed into her pajamas yet. She didn't want to turn in until Greg had returned home.

More laughter, and then the door opened.

"Hi, Mom." Greg beamed. He had a little sunburn on his nose.

Rose believed he'd grown an inch or two since leaving this afternoon. "I was getting worried."

Greg rolled his eyes.

Cam was right behind him, looking sheepish, holding a pizza box. "Mind if I come in?"

Willing her pulse to slow down but with little success, Rose motioned for him to come inside. "Please."

"Sorry we're so late." He lifted the box. "But we brought home leftovers."

"Thank you, let me give you some money—"

He held up his hand. "I got this."

"Look what Cam gave me." Greg lifted a fishing pole and a tackle box. "Mom, it was great. I caught like two fish and then when we were getting ready to go, I caught three more!"

Cam grinned. "They really started biting around dinnertime, so we stayed."

"Yeah, and then Tommy got mad at these Jet Skis. They swirled around the boat, making it rock, and he nearly fell in."

That could have been Greg falling overboard. "I knew that boat didn't look safe."

Cam laughed. "It's perfectly safe. Tommy wasn't paying attention."

She gave her son a look that forbade argument. "Why don't you put those in your room?" When he left, she turned on Cam. "You didn't have to do that."

He set the pizza box on the counter that split the living area and kitchenette. Two stools were tucked underneath. "Sure, I did. He loves fishing."

"I could see that from the picture you sent." Refusing Cam's generosity would seem mean-spirited, but his gift wasn't cheap. Taking a calming breath, she asked, "Would you like something to drink? I have lemonade and iced tea."

Cam sat on the couch and looked around, completely at ease. "Iced tea would be great. This is nice up here."

"Thanks." Rose entered the kitchenette, but peeked out between the counter and overhead cupboards. The living room area might be spacious, but Cam's presence made it seem smaller, somehow. Dressed in the same T-shirt and khaki shorts he wore at the diner, his long legs bumped against the ottoman as he leaned back.

And then there was Greg, sitting next to him, chattering about their day. Reliving it with remember-when snippets of the evening. "That was awesome. Can we go again?"

She carried in two glasses—iced tea for Cam and lemonade for her son. "Honey, don't pester. Cam was nice enough to take you tonight."

Cam reached for the glass, brushing her fingers with his. "Of course we'll go again. Greg took to fishing like he'd been born to do it. Rose, why don't you come with us next time?"

"Yeah, Mom. Can we?" Again her son beamed under the compliment.

Rose shook her head. What had she let get started? "I don't fish."

"Come on, Mom, it'll be great. I really want to do this, like when I grow up. I want to be a professional fisherman just like Cam."

"Thanks, bud." Cam ruffled her son's hair.

Rose's stomach dropped three floors. "Greg…"

"Come fishing, Rose. After I get back." Cam's eyes were awfully soft looking and earnest.

She glared back. She had plans for Greg. College plans. "No way am I getting in that boat and falling out. It looks way too fast."

Cam gave her that smile, the one that melted everything in sight, including her. "I can go slow."

The apartment suddenly seemed much too warm, even with the window fan blowing in cool night air. Rose refused to fan her face, even though she knew it had to be red. "Ah, no thanks."

Cam winked at her.

She quickly fetched an iced tea for herself, her mind whirling. Since when had she become such a stick in the mud? She'd never balked at speed before, but then, many things had changed when Kurt left her. She'd changed.

Cam tugged at her old self—the young woman who'd dressed in pretty clothes and dyed her hair wild colors simply for the fun of it. The impulsive side of her wanted to accept the invitation, but the cautious side feared the consequences. The grown-up side, which had an eleven-year-old boy to keep safe from both physical and emotional harm, didn't want to accept. She didn't want to get close only to feel the sting of disappointment when Cam decided he didn't want them. When he decided he didn't want *her* anymore.

"Come on, Mom."

She exited the kitchenette with two sets of pleading eyes willing her to say *yes*.

"We can use my parents' boat. It's older and slower and they live on a small inland lake." Cam sealed the argument with a final push. "Give me one good reason not to?"

She had many that couldn't be named in front of her son. Greg idolized the man, so much so that he wanted to walk in Cam's footsteps. Not something she wanted to see happen, but was it right to deny Greg the opportunity to fish again because of her own hangups? Maybe this new interest in fishing was a good thing. Hadn't Cam said that it had kept him out of trouble as a teen?

Taking a deep breath, Rose finally capitulated. "Okay. Okay. After Cam gets back."

"Yes!" Greg fist-pumped the air.

Rose glanced at the clock and then at Cam. "It's late. Greg, go brush your teeth and get ready for bed."

"Awww, Mom."

Rose gave her son another look.

"Okay. 'Night, Cam."

"'Night, bud." Cam stood, glass in hand, ready to leave. "Thanks for the iced tea."

"You're welcome. I'll walk you out." She had a few things to say to Cam.

"After you." Cam gestured for Rose to go down the steep stairs first.

He didn't trust the angry glare she flashed him and considered it safer to follow than lead. The thought of her pushing him over made him chuckle.

"What's so funny?" Rose said.

"The look you gave me up there. I could see you pushing me down these stairs."

Already at the bottom, Rose suddenly stopped and turned. "Yeah, about that. I really don't want you encouraging Greg to pursue fishing as a career."

"Whoa." He nearly collided with her and braced his hands against each wall to keep from teetering off the last step. He towered over her standing barefoot on the floor. Her toenails were painted a sparkling chartreuse very close in green to the plastic curly tail lures he used with jigs.

She blushed and stepped back, giving him room.

"Relax, Rose, he's only eleven."

She bristled at that. "He'll be twelve in August. And again I ask, what do you know about raising kids?"

Cam shrugged, knowing he couldn't begin to find the right words to express the feelings that had shot through him when he heard that kid say he wanted to be like him. "Absolutely nothing, but if I had a dime for every I-wanna-do-this-or-that-when-I-grow-up I heard from my brothers and sisters, I'd be a rich man."

Her mouth dropped open. "That's right. You're one of ten."

He stared at her pretty mouth a second or two.

"I'm the third one. My mother is the one who taught me how to cook. Seven of us boys had to learn, not just my three sisters. I was the only one who really enjoyed it. Although, Darren's pretty good in the kitchen with game."

"Game?" She scrunched her nose.

"Venison, turkey, grouse, rabbit, fish—you name it, and he hunts or catches it and eats it."

"Huh." Rose looked as if rallying up another argument.

"What about you? Any brothers or sisters?" Although he'd briefly met her parents, he knew so little about her background.

"One brother, older and married with two kids. He lives in South Bend, Indiana."

Cam nodded. "Good largemouth fishing near there. You know, fishing is an honest pastime. There's a youth bass fishing club in the next county. It might not hurt to check it out for Greg."

Rose rested her hands on her hips, looking feisty yet again. "I want Greg to go to college. That's why this diner is important. I've been socking away money into a college fund for him since he was born. After seeing those financials, thanks to you, I can sort of understand them. I might actually have enough by the time he graduates to pay for his tuition. First couple of years, at least."

Cam raised his hands in surrender. "Okay, I

get it. I promise I won't dissuade him from your college plans."

"Good."

He looked up to get his eyes off her. They stood in a relatively small space of an entryway lit by one overhead light fixture. The old-fashioned glass cover needed to be cleaned. He could see dead flies lying in it. He made a mental note to take care of it in the morning. To his right stood the back entrance leading into the diner and the short alley outside.

"Although, they have bass college tournaments, too. In fact, college is important even in fishing. Maybe especially in fishing because it's tough to make a living at it. There's a school near the Ohio border that has an amazing fishing team, scholarships, too."

Rose advanced on him with that glare back in full force. "You're—"

"Irresistible?" He took a step closer.

She pushed at his chest, but laughed. "Impossible. You're impossible."

He grabbed her hand and held it, stroking the underside of her wrist with his thumb. He could feel the frantic flutter of her pulse and threaded his fingers through hers. It was all he could do to keep from pulling her against him.

Could they get involved? That thought scared him as much as it tempted. Pursuing Rose meant settling down for the long haul. An image of those boxes she had stacked in the corner of her apartment came to mind, making him think about her and Greg moving into his house someday, making it more of a home.

Did he want that?

Searching her eyes, he realized part of him wanted it very much. "I care about your son, Rose. He's a good kid and I'd never steer him wrong. I hope you know that."

She gave his hand a friendly squeeze. Her eyes had never left his, as if weighing his words. His motives. Him.

Finally, she smiled and pulled her hand away. "I believe you."

"Good." He wanted her hand back, but shifted to safer ground by changing the subject. "How'd it go with Linda's attorney?"

Rose blew out her breath. "He told me I shouldn't worry about making a decision in a week. He doesn't believe the Dean boys have a strong case since Linda's will was very clear. She wasn't under any pressure or influence to change it, even if she didn't explain her reasons fully to her sons. She expressed that she wanted me to run the business right away, even before her estate was settled. He thinks I should call their bluff and he offered to notify them of my decision and then it's a wait-and-see. I'll call him when I decide for sure. Probably tomorrow."

Cam could see that her mind was already made up. She wasn't giving up her diner without a fight. Nor should she. "You're doing the right thing to keep it."

That confidence wavered. "Am I? I hope so. I pray so."

"I'll pray so, too."

"Thanks." She wore a curiously hopeful expression.

He inwardly squirmed under her searching gaze that made him all too aware of his shortcomings. The confined space where they stood didn't help, either. Two small steps was all he need take and they'd come together. What he needed was to leave before he acted on that impulse.

Being there for Greg was one thing, something he could probably handle, but could he really be all that Rose needed him to be? If he let his attraction to her get the better of him before his future was set with sponsors and a spot in next year's pro circuit, he could ruin everything.

Greg might want him to date Rose, but Cam needed to take things slow. Too many things were uncertain. If he blew it with Rose, he wouldn't be there for her son.

Maybe God wanted him to build a relationship with Greg and help the kid where he could.

Introducing Rose to his family was a big part of that. She needed to see where he came from. His parents were good people she could trust and call on if needed. Especially when he was gone on tournaments.

Cam wanted Rose to trust him, but he'd have to earn that trust.

Chapter Seven

The next morning, Rose heard Cam come in the back of the diner. She'd given him a key to the entrance off the kitchen. Hearing another voice with Cam, she turned and smiled at the older woman with him. His mother. She had classic features and highlighted blond hair pulled back into a short ponytail. They carried trays of fresh strawberries and gallons of real maple syrup that they set on the big metal table in the kitchen.

"What's with those?"

Cam grinned. "Today's special. Strawberry pancakes with Zelinsky-made maple syrup."

"I like the sound of that." Rose breathed in deep the luscious aroma of the sweet fruit and offered her hand. "Good morning, I'm Rose Dean. You must be Cam's mom."

The woman's blue eyes gleamed as she returned the handshake. The color was not nearly as brilliant a shade as her son's, but in them Rose detected excitement. "I am, and it's Helen. Cam's going to help me get up and running for the next couple of days."

Rose was floored. Cam's mom looked forward to this. "I can't even express how much I appreciate this."

Helen's smile only grew broader. "I'm glad to do it. Cam said you and your son are coming out to our place next week. Make it Tuesday and have dinner with us. And if you like the syrup, there's more where this comes from."

Rose glanced at Cam.

He winked at her. "Local ingredients are better."

"Okay, sure." Rose was definitely getting the upside of this bargain all the way around.

"Come on, Mom, I'll show you the prep station."

Rose watched them for a moment. Helen donned a hairnet, and Cam tied on his bandanna. They both washed their hands and Cam explained the process of setting up. The pride in his voice as he showed his mom what to do wasn't lost on Rose.

He loved this.

While making coffee, Rose overheard Helen whisper to Cam that she was pretty and smiled. It was a nice compliment considering she hadn't donned a trace of makeup this morning. Grinding the coffee beans and then filling several coffee filters so they were ready for the day, Rose couldn't rely on the kindness of Cam or his mom. She needed to hire a cook and soon.

While the coffee was brewing, she crossed the floor to check email on her tablet. Surely, someone had applied for the cook position. Opening her inbox, nothing was there but a forward of something silly from her dad. Two days with no hits. Not one.

Not a good sign.

"You okay?"

Rose looked into Cam's concerned-filled eyes. "No one has answered my ad for a cook."

"Give it time."

"Not something I have a lot of, I'm afraid."

With Cam's next fishing tournament in Virginia at the beginning of August, she had only a couple weeks to get a cook hired on and transitioned before he left for good. And that was if Cam stood by his offer to help with all that. What if he didn't come back?

She'd be sunk.

Her week to decide about the Deans' threat was nearly up, as well. She'd call Linda's attorney later today and request that he send word that she had no intention of selling. Rose wanted to make this work, but with so many things unsettled, she might fail in the end if she couldn't find a good cook.

"It'll be okay, Rose." Cam squeezed her shoulder. "God's in control."

She patted his hand and stood. She knew that but it didn't make her feel any better. "Thanks for the reminder. I'll get the doors. Are you ready?"

He grinned. "Oh, we're ready."

Rose lifted the Closed sign and flipped it to Open before unlocking the front door. A man waited to come in, a tall man with brown hair and bright blue eyes.

"Good morning." She opened the door for him.

He smiled and extended his hand. "You must be Rose. My name's Darren."

Accepting the handshake, Rose felt her mood lifting. "Are you here about the ad for a cook?"

He chuckled. "No. I'll leave that to my brother. I hear you and your son are coming to my folks' next week."

Cam stepped from around the counter.

Glancing between the two men, she kicked herself for not seeing the strong family resemblance. This was Cam's brother, the one who hunted and cooked *game* if she remembered correctly. "We're going fishing."

"And dinner. Tuesday," Cam added.

Darren grinned. "That's great. It's our brother Luke's birthday, so you can meet the whole family."

Rose blinked. *What?*

Cam came closer, wiping his hands on a towel. "Don't scare her out of it. What are you up to?"

"It's my day off and I thought I'd grab some breakfast before hitting the hardware store." Darren smiled at her. "What's good here?"

"Ahh." Rose couldn't seem to form two words. Dinner with Cam's parents was one thing, but the entire family? All twelve of them?

"Everything." Cam gave her an odd look and returned to the grill area, where his mother was mixing batter. "Come on up to the counter. Mom's here and we're making strawberry pancakes as today's special."

"Look at you. You're right at home here," Darren said.

"Why wouldn't I be?" Cam gave her a saucy wink.

She hadn't moved.

Neither had Darren. He leaned toward her and whispered, "You're the first woman he's ever brought to our parents' place."

"Yeah?" She didn't know what shocked her more: dinner with Cam's whole family or that she was the first woman he'd ever brought home to meet them.

Rose's nerves tightened even more. If he didn't fish well this weekend, would he consider staying? Not likely. He'd said that not qualifying for next year's series wasn't an option. He'd likely chase the next tournament after the next until he was back to where he'd been.

She fetched Darren a cup of coffee as he took a seat at the counter, her thoughts in a tangle. If she gave Cam a reason to remain in Maple Springs, would he?

Last night Cam had said that he cared about Greg and she believed him. Could he care for her, too—enough to introduce her to his parents? Enough to stay? She'd never been enough for a man to stay before...

Rose glanced at Cam, wishing she could read his thoughts and see into his heart. The bell on her door jingled. Two couples entered and sat down at a four-top table in front of the window. Rose grabbed menus and then hurried to fetch four waters. Breezing behind the counter, she grabbed four plastic cups and nearly dropped them. Cam was right there, steadying the teetering pebble tumblers by covering her hands with his own.

Her eyes flew to his. "Thanks."

"You're welcome."

The warmth of his touch surged up her arm as if she'd touched an electric fence. She pulled away quickly. Maybe she should find a reason to cancel Tuesday, before she fell head over heels for a man whose mere touch spiked her pulse.

Filling the cups with ice water, Rose considered

her options. Canceling would not only disappoint Greg, but it wouldn't help her cause to give Cam a reason to stay, if that's what she planned to do.

She watched as he served up a short stack of strawberry pancakes with whipped butter and real syrup along with a pretty, fresh strawberry garnish. Cam was good. He had a head for the financial part of the business and a creative flair with the menu. A better cook than she'd ever hope to find, but could she keep him?

During a lull in the morning rush, Cam ducked into the stairwell off the diner's kitchen to clean that overhead light he'd spotted last night before he forgot. He grabbed the step stool from under the industrial sink and placed it below the fixture.

He heard footsteps and looked up as Greg came down the stairs. "Morning, bud."

"What are you doing?"

"Cleaning this light for your mom." Cam unscrewed the glass and carefully held it while he stepped down.

The kid looked worried. "Aren't you leaving today?"

"Not till after we close. Why, what's up?"

Greg shrugged. "I don't know. Can we call you and like, see how you did?"

"Probably not a good idea. It gets pretty hectic during tournaments, but I'll give you the website where you can check the standings. Sometimes there's a video of weigh-ins at the end of the day."

Cam kept his phone with him for emergencies only. His friends and family knew not to call him unless it was urgent. He was strung pretty tight while fishing and the importance of this weekend's tournament promised to up the stress. He had to do well.

"Cool." Greg tipped his head. "Why are you doing that now?"

Cam washed it and then dried it. "I didn't want to forget."

Greg watched his every move. "Don't forget to write down that website."

Cam chuckled. "I'll do it right after this. Did you eat?"

Again, the kid shrugged. "Cereal."

Cam reattached the glass globe. "Come on up to the counter. My mom's making pancakes."

"Your mom?"

"She's going to cook for me while I'm gone and today, she's learning the ropes." Cam slipped behind the counter as Greg sat on an empty stool. He touched his mother's shoulder and she turned. "Mom, this is Rose's son, Greg. He'd love some pancakes."

His mom smiled. "Nice to meet you, Greg. My name's Helen."

Greg nodded.

"Where did you go?" His mom ladled three pools of pancake batter on the grill.

Cam looked around for a pen with no success. "I was cleaning an overhead light fixture."

"For my mom. I don't think she could have reached it," Greg added.

"Ahh." His mom's eyes narrowed on him.

He knew that look all too well. His mom was thinking, putting two and two together in her mind but coming up with six.

Cam spotted Rose breezing over to put in an order and cupped her elbow to keep her from slipping away. "I need your pen and a blank order sheet for a minute."

She handed them over, but slipped out of his grasp quicker than a bass spit back a lure. Moving toward her son, Rose smoothed back the kid's hair. "What's the plan for group today?"

Greg shrugged off her touch. "I don't know."

Cam's mom set a plate of steaming pancakes in front of the boy. "Here you go, Greg." Then she looked at him and then at Rose and smiled. "Very nice."

All he'd done was wash a light fixture, not slay some dragon. He glanced at Rose.

Her cheeks were pink. No doubt, she'd picked up on his mom's attaboy tone. He hoped Rose also noticed that his mom didn't fluster easily. She'd listened, learned and produced. His mom had once mentored him in the kitchen, and she'd already taken a couple of counter orders and waited on Greg to boot.

He quickly jotted down the website address and slipped the paper to Greg. "Here you go, bud."

"Thanks." Greg stuffed the paper in his pocket before digging into the pancakes.

"What's that?" Rose took back her pen and pad.

"A website so I can check out Cam's progress at the tournament." Greg's answer was muffled.

"Don't talk with your mouth full." Rose gave Cam that daggers look she'd given him last night.

Giving the kid a website wasn't encouraging him to pursue fishing. Although, seeing what a tournament looked like in pictures might whet Greg's appetite. If he clicked around, he'd see that there were college tournaments, too. Why was that such a bad thing?

"What?" Cam grinned at her and stepped behind the counter.

"You know exactly what." Rose put in an order with ease.

Cam switched gears. "I told you my mom was good. Not as good as me, though."

Rose rolled her eyes and returned to take another order.

"Cameron Zelinsky, what are you up to?" His

mother poured six more perfectly sized pancakes speckled with fresh strawberries onto the grill.

Watching the batter bubble around the edges, he answered with conviction, "Good things, Mom. Only good things."

More than ever in his life, he wanted to do the right thing. When it came to Rose and Greg and when it came to fishing. Especially when it came to fishing. This weekend, he'd find out what he was made of and when push came to shove in the tournament standings, Cam prayed he'd be good. Good enough to place.

Saturday afternoon, Rose locked the front door of the diner and leaned against it. She'd made it through the last three days without Cam at the grill. Helen had held her own, but she didn't have the flair of her son. Helen didn't have that care-free, bring-it attitude, either. Her food was super-good with a home-cooked, eating-at-Grandma's vibe but she turned orders out a bit slower.

All good, but not as good as Cam. His words proved true yet again.

"What a day!" Helen Zelinsky poured herself a tall iced tea into one of those glasses that Cam had brought in. He didn't like the pebbled plastic tumblers in the diner.

"You did a great job." Rose wanted to pay

Cam's mom regardless of what Cam had said, but Helen had refused.

Helen smiled. "I'm no Cam, but it's nice to know I can still muddle my way around a small restaurant."

"I wouldn't call it muddling. You know what you're doing."

"Have you had a chance to review your applications for the cook position?"

Rose nodded.

Yesterday, she had finally received two inquiries she wanted to follow up on now that they'd closed. Rose heard the telltale rattling of dishes pulled through the dishwasher. The busboy was bustling through cleanup. Was Greg still helping?

She glanced toward the back of the diner. The serviceable kitchen was not in full view; only a small portion could be seen through a narrow entry. She heard footsteps coming down the stairs.

"Mom! Cam moved up into the top three."

"You're supposed to be helping Chris."

"I was, but I wanted to check the standings real quick. Cam caught a huge bass this morning that moved him up. So far, no one's caught bigger."

Rose glanced at Helen.

"He's good." Cam's mom didn't look thrilled when she said it.

Rose wasn't thrilled at all. Selfishly, she wanted Cam to stay on as cook, but knew there'd be no chance of that happening if he did well. If she remembered correctly, there were three fishing tournaments Cam had to not only attend but finish in the top five to qualify for next year's schedule. If he succeeded, there was no way he'd consider cooking for Dean's Hometown Grille on a permanent basis.

"Want to see the video?"

"Not right now. And please help Chris in back." Rose turned to Helen. "You needn't stay. You've already helped so much, the least I can do is take care of cleanup."

"No, no. I'll have it done in a flash." Cam's mom gestured toward the kitchen, where Greg had gone. "I wonder who's more excited, your son or mine. I imagine Cam's sweating the last few hours hoping he can maintain his position."

"Is pro fishing a tough career?" Rose asked.

Helen pursed her lips into a grim line. "I've seen what the stress has done to him. He says he loves it, but after losing his sponsors last year..." She shook her head. "It really shook him up. He's not nearly as confident as he used to be."

Rose remained quiet, hoping his mom would elaborate, but she didn't.

"He loves teaching your boy to fish."

Rose chuckled. "Greg idolizes him."

Helen's smile couldn't be wider or more filled

with pride. "I noticed that. Rose, Cam might be my son, but believe me when I say he's a good man."

"Yes, he is." Rose agreed. She wasn't sure he was a good man for *her*, though. "Well, I'd better call those applicants and see if I can't get a permanent cook hired. It sounds like Cam's well on his way to success."

"I'll clean up the grill station and then call it a day." She hesitated a moment. "Rose, I really look forward to having you and Greg out for dinner with the rest of the family. Working with you these past few days, well, you're like one of my own."

Helen had a way of looking through her, right down into her heart.

Rose fought against that feeling of being laid bare along with the lump that had formed in her throat. If nothing else, she had made a true friend in Cam's mom. "Oh, Helen, thank you for that."

"You're welcome. If you ever need anything, call me. I can come back and do this again, you know."

"Thank you. I will."

Rose hoped she wouldn't need to take her up on that. She headed for her stool by the cash register and looked over the two applications. Spotting the phone number on one, she dialed it and waited. She'd set up interviews for both on Monday.

She hoped Cam meant what he said about sticking around to transition them. He'd offered his help to interview and she would take him up on that, at least. He probably knew specific questions to ask since he had the experience she lacked.

Then she would hire his replacement. The hard part was that she feared no such person existed.

Chapter Eight

Late Tuesday afternoon, Cam parked his truck in front of the diner and waited for Greg and Rose. They were headed to his parents' place for dinner. He'd been home three days and it felt good. Returning late Sunday night from the tournament in upstate New York, Cam had called Rose to reassure her that he would cook Monday. She had hit him up to help interview two applicants after they'd closed.

The timing was good. Hire on a new cook that Cam could train the following week and then step out of the picture. He needed to focus and prep for that next Open tournament in Virginia. He'd finished fourth overall in New York, but he needed to keep that trend going to qualify for next year's series. It was what he wanted. It was what he'd prayed for.

So, why didn't he feel the excitement he used to?

Rose and Greg stepped out of the front door and Rose turned to lock it. She carried a beach bag instead of her giant purse. Neither one looked his way, so he beeped the horn. The sound startled Rose but she smiled when she saw him and waved.

That smile hit him square in the chest, tightening it to the point that he thought his back might snap. He watched her approach the truck, drinking in every detail of her. She wore long khaki shorts and a sleeveless button-down top. The print was something he might see on one of his grandmother's tablecloths, but on Rose, it looked so feminine. And dangerously pretty.

"Hello." She climbed into the passenger seat and handed the bag to Greg, who had settled into the back.

"Hey, Cam."

"Hey." He nodded at the kid, then did a double take on Rose. She wore makeup again. Not a lot, but enough to notice how green her eyes looked with dark golden smudges at the corners framed by black lashes. "You look nice."

She blushed, but gave him the once-over, too. "So do you."

"Thanks." He wore shorts and a T-shirt and neither were anything special, but her compliment lodged somewhere in his midsection, making him breathe a little deeper.

There was something different in her since he'd

returned, or maybe it was him. Maybe he was different. He had never missed anyone before. Not like he'd missed Greg and Rose.

"Can we go now?" Greg moaned.

Rose's cheeks reddened even more as if she'd forgotten her son was with them. She turned and corrected him. "We don't have to go at all, you know."

Cam connected with the boy's gaze through the rearview mirror. "Hey, bud, we'll get on the lake when we get on the lake."

Greg nodded. Message received loud and clear.

He glanced at Rose. She'd buckled up and her hands were folded primly in her lap. She gave him a look of approval that confirmed he hadn't overstepped his bounds and that small gift of trust felt good. Really good.

"Do you like air-conditioning or opened windows?"

"Windows."

"Me, too." Cam rolled his window down all the way. It had been a glorious summer day, promising another mild, warm summer night ahead. He pulled out into traffic, turned and headed north, out of town.

He'd changed the radio to the same station Rose played at the diner. A soft country tune surrounded them and Rose tapped her fingers to the beat and hummed under her breath. "You like country."

She nodded. "Love it. Don't you?"

"I can take it or leave it. Although, I know a lot of the songs since it's played practically everywhere during fishing tournaments." He winked. "And at your diner."

"What do you usually listen to?"

He clicked to the contemporary Christian station. He didn't read the Bible, not like a man of faith should. He had tried, but didn't get further than a few verses before giving up, frustrated. This radio station filled the gap. For months now, he started his day on a positive note with short sermons and then music. "Believe it or not, I usually listen to this."

"I believe it." She smiled.

He smiled back.

They talked about his tournament after Greg pumped him for more information about the six-pounder he'd caught. He loved the kid's enthusiasm. Glancing at Rose, he felt his own excitement wane. She'd had a tough choice between the only two cooks that had applied and Cam wasn't thrilled with either.

One was an older guy with experience in too many chain restaurants, making Cam believe the guy wouldn't stay. The second applicant was a college-aged girl heading for a large culinary school in September. Rose had hired the latter because she wanted to continue the creativity in the menu

Cam had started. Cam didn't like her facing yet another temporary fix and told her so. Rose had simply shrugged, stating she'd cross that bridge then. *Then* was only a couple months away.

They were over halfway to his parents' place when Rose asked, "How far away do your parents live?"

"About ten miles from town. We're almost there."

Rose rested her arm along the opened window of the passenger side door. She stuck her hand outside to play in the wind and her short hair fluttered. "It's pretty out here. So many open fields. You must have rode the bus to school."

Cam groaned. "We hated the bus. Each one of us. Since we lived so far out, we were some of the first picked up and the last dropped off."

"See, Greg, you'll be able to walk to school this fall."

Cam looked in the rearview mirror. The kid played an electronic handheld game. He was old enough for a cell phone, wasn't he? Maybe he would mention it to Rose. Cam had a generous plan and it wouldn't cost much to add them.

"After-school sports will be a snap living so close. What do you like to play?"

The boy gave him a lopsided smile. "Not golf."

Cam chuckled. "You're tall. What about basketball? I think they still have a seventh and eighth grade team."

"Did you play?"

"Basketball? I sure did. All of junior high until my sophomore year of high school."

"Maybe I'll try out then."

Cam nodded, floored that this kid wanted to be like *him*.

"What happened after tenth grade?" Rose asked.

"I started the junior bass fishing circuit in earnest. I worked all summer to save up for travel costs."

"Really?" Greg perked up, but then his face fell. "But I can't fish in the winter, can I?"

"Sure you can," Cam offered. "Ice fishing is big around here."

Rose cast him an accusatory look. "I don't want him on the ice."

"Awww, Mom."

"I'm serious, Greg." Again with the mom-tone.

Cam tried to hide a chuckle, snickered, then covered it with a cough when Rose gave him one of her mom looks.

He pulled into his parents' driveway already packed with his siblings' vehicles and parked. He waited for Greg to slip out of the back seat and leaned toward Rose. "I'll take him this winter."

Her eyes narrowed. "I didn't think you'd be

around. Aren't there tournaments down South throughout the winter months?"

"Yeah, but he's not the only one I'd come home for." Cam might be getting ahead of himself but she had taken up a lot of space in his thoughts over the weekend. He wanted to know if he had a chance. If they had a chance of doing something about this attraction between them.

She searched his eyes. Hard.

"Hello, Gregory." His mom's voice sounded nearby, killing the moment.

"Just Greg," the kid mumbled.

Rose quickly looked away. She slipped from the truck and gave his mom a hug. "Hi, Helen. Thank you for inviting us. I hope your son doesn't mind us crashing his birthday dinner."

His mom laughed. "Of course not. Luke's not even here yet. Come inside and get something cold to drink. Dinner won't be for a bit and everyone's out back. I hope you brought your swimsuit."

Cam got out, too, and grabbed Rose's bag from the back seat. "Yes, we did." Rose reached for her beach bag.

"I got it."

"There's a card in there for your brother." She didn't look back again as she walked with his mom, chattering about everything and nothing, into the house.

His mom glanced his way, though, with a big fat smile.

Cam knew approval when he saw it. His mom liked Rose. Bringing her home to meet the family was a loud declaration of his intent, even if Cam wasn't exactly sure what his intentions were at this point. All he knew was that he liked being around Rose and her son. His brothers and sisters had better not remark on it, because getting involved with Rose was a big step. Big steps could lead to really big falls.

Rose sipped ice cold lemonade and scanned the huge picnic table filled with Cam's family. She and her son brought the total seated to thirteen people and there was room yet for a couple more. When Rose had asked where they found a table so large, Helen explained that her husband had made it years ago as well as the equally large dining room table.

She'd met Cam's father briefly when he stopped at the diner to look in on his wife. Andy Zelinsky was as talented in carpentry as he was at making syrup. A retired army lieutenant-colonel, the man knew how to get things done.

She glanced at Cam across from her. Greg was seated in the middle of the table, between Cam's brothers Darren and Marcus.

"It's not just about the fishing. There's the ride

up talking smack. You know, man stuff," Marcus said.

Greg's eyes were big as saucers.

Darren added, "Imagine seeing a bear swimming across a channel or moose on the shoreline. There are otters bigger than dogs up there, eagles, even cougars. You're not going to see that playing video games. We'll have to take you up there with us sometime."

As Cam's brothers filled her son's ears with tales of fishing in Canada, she knew she was doomed. Rose could envision the constant begging for the trip yet to come, and how could she dampen Greg's hopes with refusals right now, knowing there was no way she'd let him go. Unless she and Cam—

Rose slammed that possibility shut. She'd have to see where whatever was simmering between them went. He had implied that he'd come home for her, too, but Rose didn't have a good track record with long-distance relationships. Kurt had strayed—would Cam eventually do that, too? Scanning the table, she could see that Cam's family were nice people she knew she could trust. Could she trust Cam? Far too early to tell.

Cam was different at home. He seemed a little detached from his family, as if he didn't quite fit the Zelinsky mold. He joked and teased but seemed closed off somehow, not as relaxed as usual.

"Cam tells me you interviewed those two cooks and hired one. Were they good?" Helen sat next to her at the end of the table, while Cam's dad sat at the other end.

"I thought they were, but Cam didn't see it that way."

"Oh?" Helen Zelinsky's smile widened and she turned toward her son. "What was wrong with them, Cameron?"

Rose nearly laughed at the discomfort on his face.

He shrugged. "Not sure they're right for the Grille."

"It's not like I had many choices, so I went with the one I liked best. Sheila starts Monday the fifth." Rose related well to the college-aged wannabe chef. The other applicant reminded her too much of Chuck.

"Hmm. Maybe someone else will turn up." Helen leaned toward her. "No one can beat Cam in the kitchen. I hate to admit that he puts my cooking to shame."

"Oh, I don't know. This is delicious. I'd eat more but I'm stuffed." Rose patted her belly.

Although Darren had grilled the simple hamburgers and hot dogs, Helen had made the rest. She'd served homemade potato salad, a huge seven-layer salad, and a hot dish of homemade pierogi with sauerkraut and bacon that was amazing.

Helen chuckled. "We usually play horseshoes before dessert. Gets us all moving a little."

"I definitely need to work some of this off." Rose wished that she'd worn looser shorts.

"You look good to me," Cam added.

Rose felt her cheeks heat, but her skin blazed after she spotted the pleased look that passed between Helen and Andy. Darren's comment about being the only woman Cam had brought to his parents' house sunk in deeper. Maybe that was a good sign.

"Okay, let's hit the shoes." Cam's father rose from the table with a clap of his hands.

Everyone followed suit, taking their paper plates to the trash and dumping their silverware into a dishpan of soapy water. Cam had taken Rose's plate, so she gathered up the condiments and soon felt a warm touch to her elbow.

"Come on, my mom's got this. You can be my partner." Cam shifted his hand to the small of her back.

She stared into his eyes a second or two. *Partner.* The word rang through her ears like an echo. That was exactly what she wanted, but would Cam consider it?

"You okay?" He caressed her back.

"Yeah. Fine. Great." Rose tamped down the excitement bubbling within her. She skipped down the deck stairs before she leaned into his touch. "Maybe I should wait and throw with Greg."

Cam waved that idea away. "Darren's got him."

Rose followed Cam to a level area where the lawn butted up against a line of woods. Two lanes had been created, complete with sandpits and wooden backstops. Chairs were scattered about, all with good views of the area of play.

Her mind churned with possibilities. A partnership might be the perfect solution. They worked well together and if Cam became her business partner, he'd have a solid reason to stay in Maple Springs. And he could prove he could do something as good as or better than fishing. He could run a successful business with her.

If he stayed, they could be more…

It was too early for counting flowers and romance and business deals. She'd sent her refusal of the Deans' offer only this week. Kurt's brothers might yet pursue legal action as they'd threatened. It was still a wait-and-see thing. She couldn't let her heart get doubly trampled by losing both Cam and the diner. She had to be smart and take measured steps. Make sure her ducks were in a row before—

"You ever throw horseshoes before?" Monica asked with a friendly challenge ringing in her voice.

Rose nodded. "At every family picnic since I was ten."

Monica grinned. "I knew you were a good egg the minute I met you."

"Thanks." Rose didn't dare admit that she thought she and Cam were a couple at first meeting, or that she'd felt sorry for Monica's poor choice in men.

"I usually team up with Erin, but since you've got experience..."

"Back off, she's mine," Cam growled.

Rose laughed, but her stomach tipped and rolled. Too bad he'd only meant that about playing horseshoes. She glanced at Cam and shivered at the look he gave her.

Maybe they could be more.

"Come on." He steered her toward a couple empty chairs with his hand at the small of her back.

His touch felt nice. Much too nice.

Rose watched as Darren and Greg played against Cam's younger brothers, Marcus and Ben. The foursome were raucous with their teasing and Greg lapped up the male attention. He positively glowed from the praise he received when he threw a *leaner* that pushed him and Darren ahead.

"I'm so glad you're here today, as I've been meaning to stop into your diner." The woman engaged to Cam's oldest brother sat down next to her.

Rose searched her memory for the redhead's name. "Ginger, right?"

"Yes. Zach and I have the glass store farther down on Main. Have you thought about rejoining the chamber?"

"There she goes." Cam's brother Zach shook his head. "Give it a rest, would you?"

"I'm still on the membership committee." Ginger stuck out her tongue at her fiancé before turning her attention back to Rose. "As I was saying, Linda let the diner's membership lapse, but we could reinstate it for less than a new member fee. We'd love to have you as part of the Maple Springs Chamber of Commerce. There are perks, too—free advertising for one."

Rose glanced at Cam, but he shrugged. This was her decision, and until he was truly invested in Dean's Hometown Grille, she needed to quit looking to him for direction. "Sure. Reinstate me."

Ginger smiled. "Great. I'll swing by with a membership packet."

"Come on, sweetheart, we're up." Zach called for Ginger to play against Darren and Greg.

Rose caught her son's eye and smiled. "Way to go, Greg."

"Thanks."

Surrounded by these strong Zelinsky men and women, Greg thrived. He laughed a lot, too. They were a good influence for her son.

"Any word on a new sponsor?" Cam's father slipped into the seat next to him.

"Soon, I hope. This weekend's placement helped. My manager's talking with a large electronics company. Same brand I use for my GPS and fish finders. It's a good start. If I land something big, the smaller sponsors will follow." Cam sounded confident.

Of course he was. Rose had seen that room filled with trophies and excitement. Would her partnership idea stand a chance if Cam got his big sponsor?

The stability of family and a good future was all she'd ever wanted for her son. With Cam she saw glimpses of that but once the novelty of playing Dad wore off, would Cam feel boxed in and bolt like Kurt?

Greg needed this and she did, too, but in the end it would be up to Cam needing them back to make it last.

Cam offered Rose a graphite pole set up and ready to go. "This is a spinnerbait and it's pretty easy to use. Just cast like I showed you and then reel it in. It's pretty weedless so you shouldn't get too tangled up. If you feel a hit, pause for a second to let the bass get a hold of it, then jerk it to set the hook. Ready to fish?"

"I suppose." She didn't look ready, but reached for the pole.

Greg had cast three times since they'd stopped his parents' boat. The kid went straight for the top water lures, looking for the excitement of surface hits. Greg had a knack for fishing bass, all right.

They had plenty of room in the eighteen-foot pleasure craft with a decent-size inboard motor. Cam had first driven around the inland lake because Rose wanted to see the scattered homes and scenery much to her son's impatience. Cam understood that kind of antsy feeling to get a line in the water, but this evening wasn't about rushing. They had all evening and Cam wanted to take his time and enjoy.

Cam stepped behind Rose. "Casting is all in the wrist. No need to swing your arm way back. The goal is to keep the lure and hooks out of the boat."

"Like this, Mom. See?" Greg demonstrated a perfect cast.

Rose nodded and gave it a try. The lure went nowhere because she'd failed to open the bail like he'd showed her.

Cam pointed. "You've got to release the line here. Open the bail with your finger as you cast."

She tried again and the lure went no farther than a couple feet into the water. "Okay, what am I doing wrong?"

"Reel in." He stepped behind her and covered

her hand with his. Steering her aim, he gently drew back, pressing her finger down on the release. "Like this. One easy movement. Point your finger at the sky and then release the line three-quarters of the way through."

The lure sailed through the air, but Cam didn't notice how far. He breathed in Rose's scent and got lost. His fingers brushed her wrist.

"Now what?" Her voice was barely above a whisper.

He didn't answer. She might as well be fog rolling in, obscuring his thoughts and enveloping his senses. His hands slipped to her waist, resting on the slight swell of her hip. He tightened his grip when she leaned into him.

"Reel." He barely recognized his own voice.

"Fast or slow?"

"Hmm." He focused on how easy it would be to skim her neck with his lips or nibble the curve of her ear.

She suddenly jerked the pole back, nearly knocking him in the nose. Then she giggled. "Oh, no. I think it's stuck."

He watched the line dart sideways and for the life of him couldn't figure how she'd caught a fish. "Easy now, you've got a fish on. Reel in to tighten up the slack, but let it run a bit. Feel the fight."

"You got one, Mom!" Greg joined them.

She laughed when the bass surfaced with a splash. "Wow, look at that!"

Cam stepped back and enjoyed watching her bring her fish closer to the boat. "Looks like a nice smallmouth. You got it. Don't horse it, now. Bring it in easy, so you don't lose it. That's it."

He leaned over the side of the boat, grabbed the line and then picked up the bass by its mouth. "Greg, hand me those pliers, would you?"

Greg did as asked.

Cam dislodged the hook with ease and laid it out on the measuring stick before holding it out to Rose. It was maybe two pounds or so. "Sixteen and a half inches. Nice fish."

"My first one! That was pretty fun." Her excitement was contagious.

He laughed, loving this moment. "I don't know how you did it, but keep doing it. Now you know why I chase bass. Here, hold this and I'll take a picture."

Rose scrunched her nose, then turned to her son. "You do it, Greg."

"No way, Mom. This one's yours."

"Okay." Rose didn't sound too certain, but held out her hand. "Will it bite?"

"No. Tail might wiggle." Cam chuckled. "Grab its mouth here, like so."

He grinned when she held it out with two fingers. One wiggle and that bass was hitting the floor. He raised his phone and clicked.

"Now what?" Rose still held the fish as if she could barely stand the feel of it.

"Put it back in the water."

She tossed it over the side of the boat.

Cam tipped his head. "Gently, Rose. Gentle."

She scrunched her nose. "Oops, sorry."

He checked the photos. The images of both Greg and Rose each holding the first fish they caught tugged at something deep inside him. It was more than pride in teaching them how to fish. It was the way they looked at him, the way they smiled with wonder. It twisted sharp and sweet. He wanted more outings like this. Many more.

"Let me see." Rose peered over his shoulder.

"I'll send them to your phone."

"Thank you." She squeezed his arm.

"Sure, no problem." He looked at her.

Her face looked sun-kissed from being outside all evening. He'd have added his own kisses if Greg had not been with them. Out here on this inland lake loaded with bass, he should be casting, working the shallows and getting some much-needed practice hours in, but he didn't want to.

Tonight wasn't about fishing. Not really. It was giving something of himself to Rose. On some level he wanted to show her who he was and why he did what he did, hoping she'd like it, too. Hoping she'd like him.

All he knew was that he didn't want this to end. He didn't want to drop Rose and Greg off at the diner and then head home alone to his empty house. He didn't want an empty life. Not anymore.

Running from his failures, he'd kept up the pretense that he was a winner. He'd fed that fiction by doing whatever it took to earn points at tournament time. He'd never return to those old habits no matter how tough it got. This past weekend had been great, the fishing exhilarating, but part of him knew tournaments could be a bundle of nerves and frustration when things didn't go right. Part of him didn't want to return to that world even though he knew he had to.

"What?" Her eyes were soft and questioning.

He shook his head. "Nothing. Come on, there's more fish to catch."

"Tell Mom about where you and Tommy stayed while you were fishing in Canada," Greg goaded. "The one where the shower sprayed water all over your bed."

Cam chuckled and humored the kid with the quick tale told many times about the crazy motel room with a bathroom that wasn't more than a cubicle with walls that didn't reach the ceiling.

He and Tommy had filled the boy's head with stories of their many fishing trips. Rose laughed, too, but the story had lost some of its shine. That was the last time he'd gone to Canada with his brothers and cousin. Things had been going downhill for a while and then he'd been disqualified for fishing after dark, after practice hours had ceased. The reality was that he'd caught a slob of a winning bass during practice and had tried to hide it so he could retrieve it later, during the tournament.

They settled into silence and fishing, each at their own spot on the boat concentrating on the next cast, the next lure and landing the next fish. The drift was perfect, but Cam's mind wandered.

He'd excelled at fishing once upon a time without having to cheat. Cheating had been the crutch he had used to get by in school, keeping the shame of his reading level secret. He'd let Rose know about his issues. Sort of. He hadn't told her how bad it really was. He had been too afraid to accept her offer of help for fear she'd think less of him.

She deserved a man who could provide for her and Greg and wouldn't let them down. Could that man be him? Maybe, with a new sponsor. Or maybe the pressure would be even greater. Fishing to support a family was something he'd never wanted before. Could he do it now?

With God, all things are possible.

It was a snip of a scripture he had heard all his life. He'd heard it on the radio, too. Many times.

Cam knew this wasn't something he could do on his own. He'd been there, done that and it hadn't worked. Not in the end, after losing nearly everything.

He glanced at Rose, casting like he'd taught her. She laughed with her son and they teased each other. Clearly, she enjoyed this. Like she'd had fun throwing horseshoes. Rose fit well with his family. His mom already loved her and had given him a nod of approval that said Rose was a keeper.

He'd known that the minute he'd spotted her. The big question was did he have what it took to keep her? Forever.

Chapter Nine

Later that night, Rose regretted that the drive back to the diner had seemed so short. They'd laughed about their evening of fishing. After tonight, she felt part of the Cam and Greg club. "So, you're really going to cook that thing?"

Cam pulled into the back alley and parked. "It's a turkey."

"I know, but it's summertime." Rose thought he was crazy for taking the huge fresh turkey from his parents so he could use it for a special this week.

"Wait till you see what I do with it. My mom was going to freeze it. I couldn't let her kill all that flavor."

Rose shook her head. "I don't think I've ever had anything but frozen."

"Fresh is juicier and, well, fresher. Plus it's from a local farm." He gestured toward the back seat. "Greg, grab those leftovers for you and your mom."

"Okay."

"Just the pierogi, Greg. Leave the potato salad for Cam." Rose unlocked the back door, flicked on the light and dropped her beach bag near the stairs.

Cam hefted the turkey under his arm and followed them inside the diner kitchen, where he stashed the bird in the fridge.

Rose didn't want to think about how recently that turkey had been walking around. Cam encouraged her to buy as much as she could locally, but she still ordered from a food salesman that Linda had used.

"'Night, Cam. Thanks for fishing." Greg yawned.

"'Night, bud."

Rose thought she saw her son look between them and then smile, but wasn't sure. She and Cam both watched Greg dart up the stairs, leaving them alone.

An awkward silence settled between them, so Rose said the first thing that came to mind. "I can't believe he's turning in this early."

Cam rubbed the back of his neck, looking uncomfortable. "Yeah."

Rose wasn't going to drag this out even though part of her wanted to do just that. "Thank you for this evening, for fishing and your mom and family and, well, everything."

"You're welcome, Rose." There it was, that caressing sound in his voice that made her knees feel weak.

"It's late. I'd better turn in, too. Good night, Cam." Rose backed away.

"Good night."

She was equally relieved and disappointed when he left. She heard him lock the door and raced up the stairs. Her pulse hadn't quite settled back to normal yet.

After spending the day at Helen and Andy Zelinsky's large home with its large deck and long picnic table, her apartment seemed small and inadequate. Was it so bad to want a home of her own with a husband who'd love her enough to stick around?

Rose squared her shoulders, searching for a more grateful attitude, but came up empty-handed. Kurt had robbed Greg and her of days like today filled with family life. She slumped onto the couch and remembered the tickets in her pocket.

She pulled out two tickets to the chicken barbecue held by Cam's church only days away. "Hey, look what Cam's mom gave me. With the Fourth of July on a Sunday, the diner will be closed and we can go before the fireworks. Maybe even attend the parade, too. Doesn't that sound like fun?"

Her son downed a glass of milk. "Is Cam going with us?"

"Oh, I don't know. I didn't ask him."

"Can I ask you something?"

"Sure, what is it?"

Her son sat next to her on the couch. "Do you like him?"

His voice sounded pensive and terribly serious, so Rose looked him in the eyes and stalled. "Cam? Why do you ask?"

Greg shrugged. He sat very still as if gathering his thoughts for another question, as if something gnawed at him.

Rose sat up straighter. "What's this all about?"

"So, like, if he asked you out, would you go?"

"Gregory Michael, what are you talking about?" Rose felt her insides teeter. Was this coming from her son or— "Did Cam put you up to this?"

"No." Greg's nervous expression confirmed that.

"Then why?"

He stood up, irritated. "I don't know, Mom. I just wondered, okay?"

He shook his head and walked away, mumbling something that sounded a lot like *forget I even asked*.

Rose blew out her breath in a whoosh. Closing her eyes, she tried to quiet her heart, but it was racing something fierce. Hadn't she been hoping?

But why would Greg ask such a thing? Unless he wanted Cam to be part of their lives, too. Permanently, like her.

Gathering her courage, she got up and went to her son's room. Knocking lightly on the door that was slightly ajar, she waited.

Nothing.

"Greg, can I come in?"

"Yeah."

She opened the door wider but didn't step inside beyond the wall of tension emanating from her boy.

Greg sat on his bed playing the handheld electronic sports game he'd received from his grandfather last year for his birthday. Rose wasn't a fan of video games. She'd prefer Greg to read a book. She insisted the computer be kept in the living room because she didn't allow the bigger PC video games at night. Something about all that adrenaline seemed like a bad idea before bedtime.

Greg hadn't picked up the electronic game once while they were at Cam's parents'. He had been too busy with Cam's brothers and their antics. Her son hadn't been shy or quiet. He'd slipped in with the Zelinsky family like he belonged there.

Taking a deep breath, Rose gently asked, "What would you like me to do?"

Greg shrugged.

"Greg. Do you want me to go out with Cam or not?"

He looked hopeful and awfully determined for an eleven-year-old soon to be twelve. "Yeah. I do."

Rose's stomach took a tumble. She wasn't about to share her similar hopes with her son, but she didn't want to shut the door on the possibility, either. "Well, I haven't been asked."

The left side of Greg's mouth lifted ever so slightly, and he nodded.

"Did you brush your teeth?"

"No, but I will." Greg dragged himself up and went into the bathroom.

Rose rolled her head to stretch her neck but couldn't loosen the nerves bunched there.

Driving back to town, Cam had sounded excited about his upcoming two tournaments. One was in the beginning of August and the other was in September, after school started, but she couldn't remember where. Maybe Greg would know now that he followed Cam's career.

Regardless, Cam wouldn't be around for long, and she wasn't sure of his plans for the fall. Once he returned to professional fishing, would Greg's enthusiasm for the man wane or would her son simply become another fan following Cam online? Would Cam's positive influence on Greg eventually wear off, too? Right along with his interest in them? Maybe.

Unless she gave Cam a good enough reason to stay. It kept coming back to that.

The next day, Cam whistled as he walked home from the diner. Working there was pretty good. He missed prime fishing time practicing on various inland lakes, but he liked cooking for Rose. He liked planning the menus and seeing her eyes light up when he shared his special of the day with her.

He'd stayed later again to help with inventory and put away the food order Rose had received. Good thing, too. With as many folks vacationing this week as next, they'd gone through a lot of supplies already.

A hot breeze shifted the leaves on trees and rippled the American flags posted along Main Street for the upcoming Fourth of July weekend. The sun blazed above and people filled the sidewalks, making even more heat. Tourists shopped and families hit the ice-cream parlor after a day at the beach. It was the height of summer in Maple Springs.

He'd missed many a Fourth of July at home. This time of year, if he wasn't fishing out East, he'd be working events like fishing expos and the like. He'd had no series events this year after last year's disqualification had landed him at the bottom of the pile.

It had never mattered if he came home or not,

but this Fourth of July was different. He looked forward to taking Greg and Rose to the parade and then the church barbecue. Hanging out on the beach afterward until the fireworks started sounded like fun, too. He simply needed to ask.

After spending all day with Rose and Greg at his parents' place, he hadn't tired of their company. Not once. He didn't make connections like this, especially with women. He certainly didn't hang out much with kids, either, other than recently volunteering for two days with his cousin's youth program.

Turning off Main, Cam spotted Greg walking ahead of him and jogged to catch up. "Where are you headed in such a hurry?"

Greg looked startled, then smiled. "Your house."

"Everything okay?" Something had to be up for the kid to seek him out at home.

The kid nodded. "Yeah."

Cam didn't quite believe him and stopped walking. "So, what is it?"

The kid took a deep breath. "I've been invited to go camping with Jeff."

"Jeff?"

"A friend from the program. They're camping across the bridge and I want to go but…it's this weekend."

"And that's a problem, because…?" Cam wasn't

sure why the boy would seek him out on this. Hadn't he asked Rose?

Greg kicked at a crack in the sidewalk. "I don't want to leave my mom alone on the Fourth of July."

"I see. So, you haven't asked her yet?"

"No." Greg shook his head. "Will you do it? You know, maybe ask to take her."

Cam narrowed his gaze. "To the fireworks?"

Greg smiled. "Yeah. I know if you asked, I could go camping."

"She might say no."

"No. Not if *you* asked." Greg looked more than hopeful—he looked confident.

Cam chuckled. He couldn't blame the kid for paving his way to success. "When do you want to do this?"

Greg shrugged. "The sooner the better."

"Right." Cam checked his watch. It was early yet, but close enough to dinnertime. "Why don't we call your mom right now?"

Greg gave him a shrewd look. "Maybe she should meet us at your house, so you can ask her in person."

And make it harder for her to refuse. He had to give the kid credit for knowing his mom. "How about dinner?"

Greg grinned. "Yeah."

Cam pulled out his phone and called Rose, but he kept his gaze fixed on her son, who listened intently.

"Hey, Cam."

"Greg is with me and we were wondering if you'd like to meet us at my house for dinner."

A stretch of silence.

The kid's brow furrowed deep.

"Rose?"

"Yeah, I'm here. What can I bring?"

"Just yourself. See you in a few." Cam turned to Greg. "We're going to do this together, got it?"

"Yeah, sure."

Greg's steps picked up as they approached the house. The boy chattered about the upcoming camping trip with great views of the bridge. "Jeff said we'll be able to see a bunch of different fireworks from their campsite."

They were no doubt staying close to shore, which narrowed the places down. Maybe the Straits State Park. Cam had been there when he was a teenager. "What's Jeff's last name?"

"MacMillan."

Cam nodded. He'd met Jeff MacMillan Senior at the canoe outing. They'd both helped out as chaperones. Seemed like a nice guy. His cousin John would know better if Greg would be in good hands. Cam would check on that.

"Any requests for dinner?"

Greg tipped his head, considering. "Cheese-burgers?"

"You'd eat one every day if you could, wouldn't you?" Cam chuckled.

"Yeah."

"Okay, you got it then."

"Thanks, Cam. You're the best."

Warmth filled him, so he ruffled the kid's hair. "You, too, buddy."

The evening suddenly looked a whole lot brighter, knowing he'd share it with two people who'd come to mean more to him than he ever expected.

"What can I help with?" Rose stood in Cam's kitchen once again. This time, she watched him make burger patties instead of grilled steak. He added a pinch of spices to the ground beef before shaping, like he'd done a thousand times at the diner.

The three-block walk to the house had given her plenty of time to think after hearing Cam say that her son was with him. No doubt Greg had put this together and Rose could only guess what he'd told Cam. Enough to wrangle another dinner invitation, but what else?

"I thought we'd eat outside on the deck. Gather whatever we'll need from the fridge. Greg already set the table. I've got my mom's leftover potato salad and some chips, as well."

There'd be no béarnaise sauce made today. "A nice simple meal. I've actually fried a hamburger before."

"Would you like to take over?" Cam asked.

"No way. She'll burn it." Greg came in from the deck.

"Whoa, Greg, that's pretty harsh." But Cam's eyes shone with mirth.

Rose appreciated Cam coming to the rescue, but her son spoke truth. "I've burned many a frozen patty in my day and I don't have a clue how to grill. My father always took care of that."

Cam washed his hands and then grabbed a couple small zucchini. "I could teach you."

Remembering how nervous she'd been when Cam tried to teach her how to whisk, Rose shook her head. "No. That's okay."

"Greg, could you go into the garage and grab some pop from the fridge and take it out back? Here's an ice bucket—fill that up, too."

"Sure."

Rose watched her son leave, then turned her attention to Cam at the sink. He cut the ends off the zucchini and then thinly sliced them.

"I was thinking…" He paused, looking serious.

Rose braced for what might come next. Did it have anything to do with Greg seeking him out?

Cam quit slicing and looked at her. "If your offer to help me read still stands, I can help you cook better."

Her insides pitched. That would take time. A lot of time spent together. He only had two tournaments the rest of the year, maybe… "When would you like to start?"

"Right now. In the lower cupboard where you're standing, there's a grilling basket. Grab that and I'll show you an easy way to grill vegetables."

She searched and held up the small, sort of flat metal basket. "This one?"

"That's it. Normally, when I grill zucchini, I make long strips and throw them right on, but this will be easier. Here, slice this red pepper, and I'll cut the onion."

Rose fetched a small cutting board, and then cleaned the pepper of seeds and sliced it like she would for a garden salad.

"That's good. Now throw them together in the basket, drizzle with some olive oil, salt and a dash of black pepper and it's ready for the grill."

"How much olive oil?" She'd covered the veggies with a bit of salt and pepper.

"A little less than you'd use for a salad."

She nodded and followed his instructions, adding a dab more. "I don't know. You make it look easy."

"Thank you." He grinned as he grabbed the tray

filled with condiments and potato salad, chips and buns. "Bring the plate of burgers and veggies and let's go grill."

Grilling was a lot easier than she'd thought. For one thing, Cam's grill had better flame control. The burgers sizzled with brief flare-ups of fire, but nothing like the inferno of her parents' grill. So, obviously the right utensils and equipment played a role.

Cam arranged the burgers on one side and the basket of veggies on the other, then closed the lid.

"So, that's it?" Her father used to make a fuss about the importance of manning the grill, keeping close watch and constantly flipping the meat.

"That's it. We'll check on it in a bit." Cam poured a fizzy glass of pop. The ice cubes cracked as he handed it to her.

"Thanks." Rose took a sip. She glanced from the pretty table with an overhead umbrella shielding the mesh seats from the hot sun to the deep backyard that was outlined by a hedgerow of bushes. His back deck and yard looked bare, but she saw potential. "It's peaceful out here."

Cam stood next to her. "Yeah, I think so."

"Room enough for a small garden." Some yard decor even.

"Hmm. Yeah, maybe. Or more roses." He winked. He was always winking at her, teasing her, making her pulse skip.

Cam didn't look like a gardener, and reality had a way of slipping in. "You don't use all this much, do you?"

"Not really. I grill when I'm home, but it's not like I entertain or anything."

"You need a dog," Greg piped up.

Cam laughed. "Right."

"Don't you like dogs?" Rose would love to have a dog, but not now, not living in the apartment over the diner.

Her parents had a small terrier mix that had followed Greg around like a puppy. Her son was the only one who'd throw a ball for more than a few minutes.

"I love dogs, but I was never home enough before—" Cam didn't finish the statement. "I'd better check the grill."

Rose closed her eyes and hoped.

It didn't take long for the burgers to cook. Cam only flipped them once, explaining that they stayed juicier that way. The charbroiled aroma made her stomach rumble as she watched and learned. The veggies looked as good as they smelled, with slight grill marks on them. With the basket, nothing was lost to the flames below. Cam dumped the contents into a bowl and handed it to Greg to place on the table.

When they sat down to eat, Cam bowed his head. "Let's pray."

He recited the same singsong prayer he had before. It was the same one his family had said in unison at yesterday's cookout, too. Once finished, he passed the plate of cheeseburgers.

Rose accepted it, taking one, but she was curious. When it came to his faith, how serious was he? "Do you always pray that specific prayer before meals?"

"Grace? Yeah, why?"

Rose shrugged. "Do you ever pray free-form? You know, like just talking to God?"

"Sure, but those are quiet prayers."

Rose smiled at that answer. Cam had depth.

"These are good. Mom, I can't believe you helped make these." Greg took another huge bite.

"Thanks. Never too old to learn something new, I guess." Rose took a bite of her cheeseburger, but her gaze connected with Cam's. What were those quiet prayers of his? Could they include her and Greg?

"Yeah, about that." Cam nodded toward her son. "Greg's got something to ask you."

Rose turned toward her son. "You do?"

He shifted in his chair. "Ummm. Jeff MacMillan's mom invited me to go camping with them this weekend. Can I go?"

Rose leaned back in her chair. "Who is Jeff MacMillan?"

Greg looked to Cam for help.

"They are a family at church. I've met Jeff Senior. He seems like a good guy."

"Yeah, and Cam said he'd take you to the fireworks."

Rose glanced between the two of them. So, this is what Greg's *matchmaking* the night before was all about. Her son knew how much she looked forward to watching the fireworks over the bay. Did he really think she'd refuse his camping trip because of those fireworks? She'd have gone by herself, no problem, but going with Cam would be special.

They had it all worked out.

"I'll need to talk to Mrs. MacMillan."

"So, I can go?" Greg prodded.

"As long as you give me her phone number. I want to meet her before you leave." Rose wasn't taking any chances.

"Yessss!" Greg gave a pointed look at Cam.

Cam nodded, perfectly at ease, as if this wasn't a big deal. "I'll call my cousin John and get the scoop. You and I could make a day of it. Catch the parade, church barbecue and then the fireworks."

Rose willed the butterflies in her stomach to stop fluttering and hoped she sounded casual. "I have two tickets. Your mom gave them to me."

"Then it's a date." Cam smiled.

Her spine stiffened. She'd sworn off dating until Greg was much older. But with one glance at her son's pleased face, Rose knew better than to refuse. Nor did she want to.

Rose smiled back. "Yes. I suppose it *is* a date."

Chapter Ten

The next day, the diner was busier than ever. Folks poured into town for the Fourth of July weekend even more so than he remembered. They poured into Dean's Hometown Grille, too. The diner was set up to seat thirty-eight comfortably with room for forty, but his last count had been forty-five. Rose and Jess were maneuvering around extra chairs that had turned four-tops into six.

His phone buzzed from inside his pocket for the second time in the space of half an hour. He let it go to voice mail. Flipping a large order for half a dozen burgers, Cam didn't have time to check and see who had called. Not now anyway.

He finished building today's special—a turkey club paired with thick bacon and avocado along with a side of potato salad he'd made this morning after slipping that fresh turkey in the oven. He'd given the air-conditioning a workout. Cam rang the bell. "Order up."

Rose approached. "Thanks."

"You're welcome." He gave her a warm smile and enjoyed the rosy glow that covered her cheeks. He liked making her blush and it was far too easy to do. He watched her walk away and listened to her laugh at something an old guy said as she delivered his order.

Cam loved it when Rose laughed.

"Cam, hey. Dude!" Jess waved her hand in front of his face.

"What?"

She shook her head. "You two really need to go out or something. I have two more specials. Do we have enough for the next hour before close?"

"Plenty." Cam hoped he had enough fresh cut turkey to last. "And we are going out."

Jess hadn't heard the last part. She'd already hurried to the next table needing their order taken.

He rubbed the back of his neck. This *date* loomed like a tournament he *had* to win. Rose didn't seem the least bit pressured by it. This morning she'd teased him in that friendly way of hers, calling him crazy once again for cooking a whole turkey on what promised to be a hot summer day.

Returning to the grill, Cam plated four cheeseburgers and two deluxe hamburgers. With Greg heading to camp after program tomorrow, maybe he should ask Rose to dinner or take her out on his boat to catch the sunset to take the pressure off Sunday. Neither idea sounded casual enough.

He'd put off reading together, but maybe he should rethink that, too. Friday night might be the perfect time, but when she realized how badly he read, would she change her mind about spending the day with him Sunday?

He blew out his breath. Greg's camping request had come along and opened up the door for Cam to make good on Rose's offer to help. Reading would make it more of a casual thing, too. Casual was good. Smart. Safe.

Cam slapped the call bell, announcing the large order of burgers was ready. His phone buzzed again and moments later it whistled with an incoming text. This time he checked, scanning a text that came from his business manager.

Good news. Call ASAP.

He read the first line over again. He'd been waiting to hear good news for months—

"Everything okay?"

He focused on Rose's concern-filled eyes. "Yeah. Why?"

"You look like you just got bad news."

"A text from my business manager." So why wasn't he more excited?

Her face fell. She didn't look excited, either. "Oh?"

He glanced at the clock. They closed in half an hour, but with this crowd, they wouldn't have everyone out by then. Not by a long shot. The bells on the door announced more people coming in.

Cam reached out for the order ticket Rose held. Work now, good news later. "What's next?"

"Another two specials."

He grinned at her. "The turkey club is a hit."

She nodded. "Okay, okay, you were right."

"Of course I was." He chuckled as she quickly grabbed four menus and headed for the latest customers.

The following hour flew. When every customer was finally gone, Cam cleaned the grill and prep station, but didn't offer to do more. He had a phone call to return.

Catching Rose's attention at the cash register, he mouthed the words, "I've got to go."

She nodded, and so he left, hitting the return call button as he went.

"Took you long enough to return my call."

"I was working." Cam barely missed a group of teenagers who suddenly stopped walking and pointed at a storefront window.

Bob snickered. *"You're cooking at a diner, right?"*

"That's right. So, what's your news?"

"Got a big technology company that wants to meet you. Dinner tomorrow night and we'll seal the deal."

"Whoa, hold on." Cam ran a hand through his hair. "When and where?"

"I emailed you a flight schedule. You can fly out of the Pellston airport tomorrow morning and pick up a connecting flight in Detroit. That'd get you into Kansas City in time for dinner in Olathe."

Cam's head spun. He couldn't leave tomorrow. He couldn't leave Rose hanging, not on the busiest weekend of the summer. There was his promise to Greg, as well. The kid didn't want Rose alone for the fireworks. "Can't do tomorrow."

"What!"

"I'm needed here the next three days. Make the same arrangements for Monday, the fifth." The day the new cook started.

Silence.

"Bob?" Cam stepped off the sidewalk and stopped near Center Park.

"You use their GPS and sonar technology and always have. Do you realize what a perfect situation this is? In no time, you'll be right back in the groove with other sponsors jumping on board. I've got a call in to an iced tea company, too."

It didn't feel perfect, but Bob was right. With a big name backing him, Cam had a good chance

of signing more advertising sponsors. Maybe even
re-sign some that he'd lost. "I need a couple days."

*"Cam, if you wait, you might lose this oppor-
tunity."*

He considered that. For years, he'd jump at
chances like this, feeling like a beggar. He was
tired of it. At thirty-four, maybe he was tiring of
the struggle to stay near the top year after year.

He closed his eyes and focused on God and
the deal they'd made. This was the answer to his
prayers. Refusing didn't seem like a good idea
and yet he had responsibilities here that he wasn't
going to shirk.

"If these guys can't wait a couple days, then I
don't want to represent them." A sense of peace
filled him. It was his career and he'd made the
call. A good one.

He heard Bob sigh. *"Okay. Who is she?"*

"She?"

*"I wasn't born yesterday. There's got to be a
woman involved for you to give up a golden opportunity so you can stay home and play house?"*

Cam tamped down the blistering retort poised
on the tip of his tongue. He wasn't playing. He
cared for Greg and Rose. He cared a lot. Enough
to want things he never thought he could have.

"I'm not giving up anything. I'm asking for a
weekend. A holiday weekend at that. Make it so
and let me know."

Bob sighed again. *"I sure hope you know what you're doing."*

"I do." Cam disconnected before he changed his tune.

He might have thrown away the chance he'd been waiting for, but he wasn't going to let Rose down. More important, he didn't want to let God down by sliding into his old ways.

Hitting another number in his contacts, Cam waited until she picked up. "Mom? I have another favor to ask you."

"What's that, honey?"

"Could you help transition the cook for me on Monday? If she's good, you needn't stay long. I'll be there for a couple hours of the morning."

"Why, where are you going?"

"To meet with a potential sponsor. A big one in Kansas."

"Are you sure that's what you want?"

Cam didn't know how his mom did it, but she cut right through to the heart of his own doubts. "What are you talking about?"

"You're more relaxed than I've ever seen you. Working at the Hometown Grille is good for you, Cameron. So is Rose."

Cam couldn't argue with that, but before he could ever hope that Rose might want to share his future, he had to redeem it. He needed to make some very wrong things right again.

"Right now, Mom, it's something I have to do."

"I sure hope you've prayed about this."

"Every day since I came home."

"Maybe I should call Rose and make sure she wants me there."

"I got it, Mom. I'll let her know and then call and confirm with you, okay? Just plan on coming to the diner around eight on Monday."

"Okay."

Cam disconnected.

Rose knew this day would come. They both did. Hiring a new cook confirmed that it was time for him to go. He'd never expected this hesitation to leave, feeling as if he had left something undone.

Friday morning, Greg ambled into the diner dragging his backpack and looking sleepy.

"Hungry?" Rose smiled at her son. She'd helped him pack for his weekend trip last night, making sure he had everything he might need. It was no wonder that backpack looked overstuffed.

"Sure." Greg dropped the backpack and grabbed a real glass for milk. One of Cam's tall glasses he used for iced tea. He sat on a stool at the counter.

"What do you want, bud? Eggs, French toast?" Cam asked.

Greg shrugged. "Eggs are fine."

The diner wasn't full this morning, so Rose

slipped onto the seat next to him. "You should have everything. Did you grab your toothbrush?"

"Yeah." He sounded irritated.

She brushed his hair back. "Be careful and listen to Mrs. MacMillan."

"Okay, Mom." Greg tipped his head away from her touch.

Rose sighed. Her baby hadn't often gone away for the weekend unless it had been with her parents. "I won't see you till Monday."

Her son nodded.

Cam finished up Greg's scrambled eggs with cheese over hash browns. He handed him the plate and her son ruined it by squirting ketchup all over the top. "Aren't you taking your fishing pole?"

"I'm going to use theirs."

Cam nodded. "Good idea."

"I'll miss you." Rose bit her lip to keep from getting really mushy.

"Awww, Mom." Greg rolled his eyes and dug into his food.

Rose glanced at Cam. He looked amused by her fussing over Greg and shook his head. He must think her overprotective, but this was the first time Greg had gone away on his own, without any family, for a whole weekend.

Rose watched her son eat, memorizing his face in case he looked different when he came home. Her son was changing fast, growing up and needing her less. Wanting her motherly hugs and snuggles not at all.

The MacMillans planned to leave for the Straits State Park after picking up the boys from the youth program. Once she'd met them, Rose knew Greg would be in good hands. They were nice people. Cam had been right about that.

He'd been right about many things—from buying local products like his parents' syrup to roasting a whole turkey in July. Cam was good at what he did. She believed that he'd increased business at the diner, so it wasn't any surprise that he'd received good news from his business manager.

She hadn't even asked what it was, knowing whatever it was would likely push Cam out the door for good. She'd dreaded the day he left the diner to pursue his fishing career. She'd hired Sheila with the hope that Cam might return in the fall. After everything was settled with the diner, maybe then she could offer him a partnership.

Linda's attorney had let her know that Kory Dean had signed for the letter they'd sent refusing the buyout offer. She'd followed the attorney's suggestion to call their bluff. It was their move now. Would they really contest?

"What?" Greg looked at her.

"Nothing." She shook off her dark thoughts and smiled. "Have fun this weekend, okay?"

Greg nodded, his mouth full.

Rose would have fun, too, even if she had to force it. She stood when Greg grabbed his plate, in a rush to be off and gone. She followed him into the kitchen. "Okay, give me a hug."

"Awww, mom."

"Hey, give your mother a hug." Cam had come in for more mayonnaise from the industrial fridge. That sure sounded like something her father might have said. It was as if they'd become a family of sorts.

Greg did as bid and Rose hung on tight. "I love you."

"Me, too," her son mumbled and let go.

Cam fist-bumped her boy. "Have fun, bud."

"Yeah." Greg nodded and left.

Rose watched him leave with a combined sense of loss and freedom.

"You okay?" Cam touched her shoulder.

"I am." Freedom won out as she looked up at Cam. "Hey, what are you doing later? Want to come over and read?"

He looked surprised and then smiled. "I was thinking about asking you the same thing."

She grinned. "I'll order takeout. No cooking. Say six?"

He nodded. "Seven is better so I can get a couple hours of fishing in."

Her hopes took a dip. Fishing came first. She

heard the bells to the diner door ring with new customers. "Seven it is. Got to go."

She didn't have time to ask about his news from the previous day. He might well have a sponsor in hand. If so, he hadn't said anything and he would, wouldn't he?

She'd find out tonight.

That evening, Cam took a deep breath and knocked on Rose's door. Tonight was about his issues with reading. He'd agreed to her offer of help, figuring that she might as well know sooner rather than later what she was up against. If he wanted a future with Rose, he could no longer hide who he was. And who he wasn't.

With Greg gone, it would be the perfect time to start. Awkward? Definitely, but not nearly as bad as having her son observe how poorly he read. Cam was probably worse than the average fifth grader.

She opened the door and smiled. "Hi."

He struggled to keep his gaze fixed on her pretty face and failed. Dressed in a light green tank top and breezy white pants that ended at her shins, Rose looked cool on a hot summer's eve. "Hi."

"Come in. Sorry, it's so warm. I don't have air-conditioning up here. We can go downstairs to the diner if you'd like. It'll be cooler. You can check that brisket you're marinating for tomorrow's special." She seemed nervous.

That made two of them. This was the first time they'd been alone, without Greg.

"Here's fine. I'll come in early to take care of the brisket. I've got a barbecue platter planned complete with corn on the cob and boiled salt potatoes with drawn butter for the special."

She tipped her head. "What are salt potatoes?"

"They're small new potatoes boiled in salt water. It's a big thing in upstate New York. I discovered them at a local fair after fishing a tournament there."

"Oh." Rose headed for the tiny kitchenette. "Iced tea?"

"Please."

He scanned the living room. The stacked cardboard boxes he'd seen before were gone. The window fan churned heavy warm air from one of two tall windows facing Main. He could see the bay from up here and dark clouds gathered in the west. They might be in for a storm. He should have driven instead of riding his bike the short three blocks from his house, but it hadn't looked that bad a while ago.

His attention snagged on a stack of books lying on the coffee table. Wiping his hands on the front of his T-shirt, he swallowed panic. Could he really do this? That stack taunted him, like the kids used to in grade school when he took forever to muddle through a page he was supposed to read aloud.

Cam pulled his phone from his pocket, hoping a return message from Bob might give him an excuse to leave. There was still nothing to report. He might have blown the offered opportunity. He leaned against the half wall of the kitchenette. Time to man up and give this reading thing a shot.

"You never told me about your good news." Rose plated aromatic cashew chicken with a side of vegetable lo mein.

"You didn't ask." There'd been nothing from Bob other than he was waiting for a call back.

"Honestly, I was afraid to." She stopped dishing up food and looked at him. Through him. "You're leaving, aren't you?"

"Not yet. My manager's working on setting something up, but nothing's been confirmed." Friday evening with no word, so Monday looked doubtful at this point.

Rose reached into the freezer and dumped a handful of cubes into a tall glass with a clatter. "Ice?"

"Sure."

There was no sense telling her that he hadn't jumped at the offer to meet because of his responsibilities this weekend. He wouldn't word it right and he didn't want Rose to think losing a sponsor was somehow her fault. Because of a date he wanted to keep.

If Cam didn't land this sponsor, it could be a long wait before another one showed interest. This would make his placement in the August tournament even more important. He'd funded his own way this year and his bank account still had a nice balance. He'd be okay. For now. But next year's pro series events were expensive. He'd need sponsors to continue.

He watched Rose's fluid movements as she grabbed the pitcher of iced tea. Given the chance to do it over, he'd make the same call. There wasn't any place he'd rather be right now than right here.

Rose caught him staring and blushed as she poured their drinks.

"We can eat here at the counter or in the living room," Rose offered.

"Living room. I want to check out those books and see what torture you have planned." He grabbed his plate and glass and headed for the couch.

Rose laughed as she followed him. "I'll go easy on you."

She sat on the couch but with a good bit of distance between them. "Chopsticks?"

He reached for the fork she also held out. "You think eating with sticks is going easy? I want to eat while it's hot."

She opened the package of chopsticks with a flourish and dug into her cashew chicken. "I've eaten a lot of takeout in my day."

"I can tell." He took another bite. The rumbling sound of distant thunder confirmed a storm rolling in off the bay. "Any word from Greg?"

"Beth MacMillan texted me earlier with their campsite number and to say that they'd made it." Another rumble of thunder, louder, made Rose cringe. "Good thing they have a camper."

Cam agreed. "Have you thought about getting Greg a phone?"

"Yes."

When she didn't say more, he prodded. "But decided against it because…?"

She shrugged. "I have to look into it. I have an older phone that's month to month, not an actual plan."

"He can go on mine. You both can."

"That's generous of you."

"Not really, just cost-effective. I have an internet, phone and TV bundle. It'd probably be cheaper to add a couple extra lines on mine instead of opening a new account."

"Cam—" Her pretty brow furrowed.

"Just give it some thought." He set his plate down and picked up a book he knew all too well.

He remembered trying to tackle *The Swiss Family Robinson* in school. Opening it to the first chapter, Cam stared at the words on the page. He tried to make the letters stop jumping around and finally gave up. He couldn't remember anything he'd ever worked so hard to understand only to give up every time, defeated.

He'd found the movie at the Maple Springs public library and that was the only way he'd passed his oral book report in sixth grade. Watching movies instead of reading books had been one of the many ways he'd skirted his issues.

"We can start with that one."

His stomach turned. "Maybe this isn't such a good idea."

Her hand touched his arm. "A couple years ago, Greg's teacher noticed his struggle with reading and recommended that he be tested. Greg is dyslexic. A mild case."

He'd heard the word before, but didn't know what it meant. Not really. "Dyslexic?"

Rose set her plate down, too. "Dyslexia can be flipping certain letters around and trouble comprehending what's read. In Greg's case, he couldn't keep letters in order. We enrolled in a special class that helped tremendously. There were adults in that class, too, Cam."

"We?"

"I went so I could coach Greg at home. He reads, not as much as I'd like, but he does read much better now. I know because I make sure his teachers know about his challenges and I ask them to forward their reading schedules to me, so I can read the books, too, and quiz Greg. He retains more than he used to."

A seed of hope cracked open. "What kind of class?"

Rose pulled a couple of large paperbacks from the bottom of the pile. They were more like workbooks and well-worn. "We learned that it's important to control disorientation with words you can't picture or visualize their meaning. Sounding out words doesn't always work for dyslexics, because they see things differently."

He leaned closer as she opened the workbook, pulled out a couple note cards and explained an exercise he could try that limited how many words he saw at a time. She encouraged him to focus on reading the letters in sequence before saying the word.

"Give it a try. Aloud, though. See if there's any difference from before."

He glanced at her hopeful face. She didn't for a minute look worried or put off by any of this. Taking the note cards in hand, he reopened *The Swiss Family Robinson*. Blocking most of the page helped the words stay put somewhat. Following the exercise she'd showed him, he could focus a bit better, but still stumbled as he read line by line.

She leaned over his shoulder and followed along.

In spite of her nearness and the softness of her voice encouraging him, he only made it through the first page. He leaned back, defeated. "It's no use."

"There's more."

Before he could ask what she meant, lightning flashed and thunder rumbled louder. The fan flickered off, back on, then off again.

"There goes the power." She got up and headed toward the window to look outside. "Now it's really going to get hot in here."

"We can do this another time." His skin itched with discomfort that had nothing to do with the stifling air. Watching the fan blades slow to a stop, he wanted to bail on her right then. He felt like an idiot.

"Oh, no. Like I said, there's more." Her eyes shone as she headed for her son's room. "I'll be right back."

Cam forced himself to remain seated on that couch. She looked too eager for him to bail on her now. What was she up to?

Chapter Eleven

Rose tamped down her excitement. Cam had to be dyslexic, much more so than Greg. It explained a lot—his creativity with food, his acumen with numbers and the reason for hiding behind his charm.

When she came out of Greg's room with a couple of cans of Play-Doh, he looked wary. "What's that for?"

She bit her lip, hoping he wouldn't refuse. "This is something we did in class. Since the power's out, we don't need that much light anyway. I want you to make the letters of the alphabet with this dough."

He snickered. "What?"

"Humor me." She wasn't backing down now. Not when she knew, not when she could prove to him that he could improve with the right tools. It wouldn't all happen tonight, but if she could simply open the door for him to consider getting help, then he was well on his way to success.

Cam shrugged. "I guess I'm in your hands, might as well go with it."

Then he opened a can and got busy making letters. *A. B. C.*

"Line them up on the coffee table, while I get rid of our plates. We'll do punctuation marks, too." She brushed against his arm when she grabbed his plate. The power might be out, but electricity ran through her veins at that simple touch.

He looked up, his eyes smoldering. He'd felt it, too.

Lightning flashed again followed by a crash of thunder that rattled the windowpanes. A strong gust of wind blew in through those opened windows, making the blades of the fan spin in the opposite direction. Papers fluttered to the floor from the computer desk behind her and then the roar of rain came, but neither of them flinched.

Rose breathed deep but it did little to calm her racing pulse. Now was not the time for romance, not when these exercises were so important. Not when Cam's welfare was more important than whatever sizzled between them. She wanted him to *want* to improve, get more help. She wasn't going to jeopardize that by falling into his arms.

"Make both uppercase and lowercase letters. I'll be right back."

Cam nodded and continued.

She dumped the plates in the sink and then lit a couple of candles. They needed more light. Rose refilled Cam's glass with iced tea before sitting back down beside him on the couch.

"This is probably slamming in way too much at once, but look over those letters and punctuation. Close your eyes and picture them."

He did everything she asked without mocking her, or flirting. He actually took this seriously and that made Rose want to whoop and holler, but she stayed quiet, watching him.

"Now we'll try the index card exercise again." Rose held her hands in her lap and waited, praying she was right.

He repeated the same page a little faster than before. As if finally finding light at the end of a dark tunnel, Cam looked at her. "I want to know more about these classes you took."

Rose wanted to cry seeing the excitement and hope shining in his eyes. "I'll find out if there are any up here. How did your teachers miss this? I mean, how'd you make it through high school without anyone testing you?"

That light in his eyes dimmed. "I was good at hiding my limitations. I'd watch the movie instead of reading the book, and I cut other corners, too." He leaned back and blew out his breath. "Friends did my homework and took tests for me."

Her breath caught. "You cheated."

His golden skin paled. "Pretty much, yeah. A bad habit I'd picked up early."

"What about your parents?"

Cam shrugged. "They didn't know the extent of it, only that I wasn't good in school. I had been labeled lazy and was told that I didn't apply myself. That was better than being called dumb, so I got by. Math kept me afloat and I managed to graduate with just barely a passing grade point average."

He'd hidden so much from everyone. "Well, that's done and over. This program will make a huge difference, you'll see."

He stared at her. "My reading doesn't bother you, or the cheating?"

"Of course it bothers me! You were young and facing all that alone when you didn't have to. Even though the signs were all there, no one figured out why you read so poorly. Contrary to what *you* might think, you're a smart man—creative and intuitive. Without your help, I would not have had near this much success with the diner."

He looked as if a weight had been lifted from his shoulders. One he'd carried far too long. He tapped the paperbacks. "Can I borrow these workbooks?"

She nodded. "Take what you want."

His gaze dropped to her lips.

Rose swallowed hard. She'd uttered dangerous words.

"Thank you." His voice was whisper soft.

She needed to get them back on task and fast. "The class is not easy, but you'll be amazed at the improvement."

"I'm already amazed."

They'd crossed a line and stepped into frighteningly honest territory. She wanted to take another step further and opened her mouth to ask if he'd consider staying on at the diner when the ringtone on her cell shattered the moment.

Glancing at her phone, Beth MacMillan's name and number flashed across her screen. "I'm sorry. It's Greg."

He smiled as she answered.

Rose breathed easier when her son said he was calling to make sure she was okay because of the storm. "I'm fine. It's just rain here now."

Another cell phone buzzed. Cam's.

She watched him read the screen while Greg filled her in, something about fishing and then eating what he and Jeff had caught. Greg was glad the MacMillans had a camper, because the storm sweeping through the Straits had been rough but pretty cool according to her son.

Cam gathered up the large workbooks along with *The Swiss Family Robinson* and stood. "I better go."

That was definitely wise, even if disappointing. "Hang on while I tell Cam good-night," she told Greg.

"Can I talk to him?" There was no mistaking the excitement in Greg's voice.

"Sure." Rose held out the phone. "Greg wants to tell you something."

Cam took the phone and after a few seconds, laughed. "That's a good-size panfish you got there. Good job."

Rose smiled. Of course they'd talk fishing. Cam looked so proud of Greg, listening intently to whatever it was that her son told him.

Her vision grew hazy and her stomach suddenly went queasy as it hit her that she loved Cam. In two weeks, she'd fallen hard.

"Got to go, bud. I'll hand you back to your mom." Cam then said softly, "See you in the morning."

Rose nodded and watched him leave, her heart a tangled mass. Now what? How could she protect her heart when she'd just given it away like a foolish girl? She could admit her feelings and desire for the future, but that didn't mean Cam would want to share those things with her. She wanted permanence and he'd only promised temporary.

Rose hummed under her breath and closed the cash register. Customer traffic had trickled off to nothing by closing time so they hadn't needed to stay late. She glanced at Cam with his messy blond hair from wearing a bandanna and her heart skipped a beat.

He caught her gawking and grinned, but his expression softened as he approached. "I think we're all set."

"Yes."

"Want to go fishing with me?"

Last night's storm had cut the heat and humidity, making today perfectly warm and sunny. A perfect day for anything out of doors, but Rose had some inside plans for the afternoon. "You go ahead. I've got some shopping to do."

"For what?"

"You'll see tomorrow." It had been a long time since Rose had splurged on herself. Considering the stellar few weeks of receipts at the diner, she could afford to purchase a few things for their *date*. Now that she knew her heart, she'd give it all she could in giving Cam a reason to stay.

He stepped closer. "I like the sound of that. Pick you up for church in the morning?"

"Can we go to mine? Service doesn't start until ten."

"Sure."

Rose wanted them to attend church together. Not only tomorrow, but many more Sundays. With Greg home next weekend, maybe he'd go again before leaving for the next tournament. A family image of the three of them in church stirred sweet like a dream come true.

Cam had once thought fishing the only thing he could do well. That was before the light at the end of his dark reading tunnel had shone. If Cam pursued those classes, his world could grow beyond fishing. Would he see the opportunity he'd have here in Maple Springs? *If* Cam accepted her offer to run the diner together. It was what she wanted, it's what she'd ask on their date. No more waiting.

His phone buzzed, so he retrieved it from his pocket. "It's my mom. I've got to take this. I'll see you tomorrow."

"Okay."

He squeezed her shoulder and left, phone to his ear.

Rose stripped off her apron and looked down at the T-shirt and jeans she wore. They'd stayed relatively clean and that was saying something considering that she'd served a lot of barbecue brisket specials that included a round cup of drawn butter for Cam's salt potatoes. She had her own plate tucked away in the fridge for later.

Right now, she had to get moving. She didn't want to be late for her first hair appointment since moving here. She needed a trim and maybe a highlight, something to brighten up her dull look. She wanted a new dress, too. Something casual yet pretty enough to make Cam want to stick around. She'd do whatever she could to make sure what had started with Cam not only grew but lasted. Forever.

Grabbing her purse, she headed out the front door of the diner, locking it behind her. When she turned, she spotted Cam's sister heading her way.

Rose waved and waited.

Monica waved back. "Hey, Rose, what are you up to?"

"I've got a hair appointment, then shopping."

"For your date with Cam?" She grinned, looking a lot like her brother.

"How'd you know?"

Monica rubbed her hands together with glee. "Cam told Mom and she told me. Can I tag along and help?"

No doubt, Rose looked like she needed help. She'd never be labeled as fashionable these days, not when she wore clothes until they wore out. Style didn't matter anymore. Considering her daily uniform of T-shirts and jeans or shorts, comfort and function had become her priority.

Rose glanced at Cam's sister. She dressed impeccably and her sun-streaked long blond hair and manicured nails were perfectly coifed. It was no wonder Monica offered her assistance. It wouldn't hurt to have some female advice she could obviously trust.

Rose looked into kind blue eyes and gave in. "Sure. Why not?"

"Great. Which salon?"

"The one around the corner." Rose hurried her steps to keep up with the long-legged Monica.

"That's where I go. They're actually a client of mine and they do good work."

When they walked inside, three women warmly greeted them. Before Rose could say a word, Monica took charge by introducing her, then ushering her to a seat with one of the three beauticians.

Rose reached out and shook the woman's hand. "Nice to meet you."

The woman grimaced when she scanned Rose's work-roughened hand. "We're running a special on manicures today."

Rose shook her head, but Monica butted in. "She'll take it. Throw in the manicure on me."

Rose pulled her hand away. "I don't need one."

"Oh, yeah, you do." Monica and the beautician chorused in unison.

The three of them laughed, but Rose stalled. She wasn't sure how to take Cam's sister, who was bossy, pushy even, but also kind.

Monica rolled her eyes. "I know, I'm sorry to prod, but Mom is hoping, we both are, that well, you and Cam... What I'm trying to say is that you're good for him and I hope you two get together."

They hadn't been on their first *official* date yet,

but it was nice to know Cam's family was in her corner. Very nice, indeed. "So, you want to be my fairy godmother before the ball?"

Monica nodded. "Yes. That's exactly it, if you'll let me."

Warmth washed through Rose. Monica might have some hard edges but she was soft underneath. "Let's hope your influence helps, because it's what I want, too."

"Good." Monica narrowed her gaze. "Now, what were you going to do with the color of your hair?"

Rose shrugged. "Highlight. Or maybe blond?"

"Honey, with your sweet skin tone, you could easily carry off platinum." The beautician handed her a picture of gorgeous white-gold hair.

A zip of daring surged through Rose as she looked in the mirror at her cap of mousy brown. She'd never liked the naturally dull color but had worn it for years now, hoping to go unnoticed. Hoping to keep her heart safe. Yet here she was, putting her heart out there one more time. They said that three times was the charm and it couldn't hurt to look her best.

Glancing at Monica, who nodded with approval, Rose squared her shoulders. "Let's do this."

All the way to church, Cam kept glancing at Rose. He'd thought her pretty the moment he first saw her, but *this* stylish woman sitting in the passenger seat made him nervous. Real nervous. Her transformation reinforced how little he had to offer her.

"What?"

"Nothing, I'm just looking at you and your hair." Her newly bleached blond hair made her lightly tanned skin glow. A good amount of that skin showed in a sleeveless dress that didn't quite skim her knees. He thought he'd seen that same outfit hanging in the window of one of the shops on Main.

"You don't like it…"

He took in the sweep of really blond bangs. "Oh, I like it. I like it a lot."

She smiled, then gasped when his tires hit the raised rumble strip in the center of the road. "Hey, keep your eyes on the road."

He chuckled and pulled back into his lane. He preferred looking at her, though. "What made you change, uh, your hair?"

"What if I did it for you?" Rose's voice was whisper soft.

Her admission slammed through him. No woman had ever made such a gesture. But then, no woman had made him create the alphabet out of Play-Doh before, either. He'd started reading those workbooks she gave him. It was a slow process, but worth it if everything he'd thought about himself might not be true.

He pulled into the church parking lot, turned off the engine and faced her. "For me, huh?"

She nodded. Her green eyes were rimmed with dark brown. Shimmery gold covered her lids. Not too heavy, but more noticeable than before.

"I think you're beautiful no matter what your hair color." He caressed her cheek, running his thumb across her bottom lip. Leaning closer, he wanted those lips against his own, when he spotted something move beyond the truck.

He shook his head and groaned at his brother Zach, making faces only a few feet away.

Ginger tried pulling him away, but failed and mouthed the word, "Sorry."

Rose turned around to see what distracted him and blushed. "Nice."

"Real nice." Cam's opportunity to ask why she'd done this for him passed, right along with a perfect chance to finally kiss her.

He watched Rose slide out her door. The strappy leather sandals on her feet matched the belt she wore cinched around her trim waist. His gut twisted. Man, she was beautiful.

"Love your hair," he heard Ginger tell Rose. The two chatted about their respective business traffic for the week as they entered the church.

Sliding into the pews, Cam reached for Rose's

hand when he spotted a couple guys checking her out. She could have anyone. Would she really be happy with him? Knowing his limitations hadn't stopped her from coloring her hair. *For him.*

She threaded her fingers through his and didn't let go, even when they stood to sing.

Cam soaked in the song service. It was definitely longer than what he was used to, less formal, too. The sanctuary was simply appointed with tall windows that were topped with blocks of colored stained glass. Nothing ornate like his church. Three of his brothers went here now and Cam could see why. There was something inclusive about this church, something warm and welcoming.

As he listened to the message, Cam's ears rang as if it had been given for him. The minister spoke about living out faith publicly and with courage. He had read from the first chapter of the Book of Joshua and the words hit hard.

No one will be able to oppose you as long as you live, for I will be with you, as I was with Moses; I will not abandon you or fail to help you. Be strong and brave...

The rest of the verses read aloud were lost to Cam because that first verse echoed through his soul, over and over again. Instead of growing faint, it grew louder. He stared at the sermon note page that had been stuffed inside the bulletin. Zeroing in on one letter at a time, he realized that same verse was on there, in bold letters.

Cam folded it and tucked the page into his back pocket. He needed to read that verse over and over until he knew it by heart. God had spoken. To him. And he needed to listen.

As the minister wrapped up his sermon, Cam spotted Darren a few pews in front of them. He sat with Bree, his girlfriend, who'd flown in from Seattle for this past week. Those two sat close as if clinging to each other, knowing they'd soon say goodbye.

Cam glanced at Rose. Her head was bowed and her eyes closed as the minister prayed over the congregation, dismissing them for a blessed day.

He'd heard back from his manager and Monday's meeting was a go. He'd be gone a couple days, three at the most. Cam bowed his head, too, but couldn't focus on the prayer. He needed to tell Rose about the upcoming sponsor meeting. He should have said something to her yesterday, after he'd received a call from his manager on Friday night confirming flight information. He'd planned to tell her today, but then seeing her hair and makeup had knocked him for a loop.

Last night, after fishing for hours, he'd worked through another exercise from those workbooks. He wasn't sure if he'd done it right, but he'd do what he could to improve. He'd made a promise to be a better man, but could he be? It felt like he was heading for the lion's den tomorrow, meeting with a potential sponsor.

"Cam?"

He looked up. People were leaving. Church was over.

"Everything okay?"

"Yes." He'd tell her later. Right now, he wanted to enjoy the day. Exiting the church, he took hold of Rose's hand once again. "Ready for the beach?"

"I am." She flashed him a saucy smile. "I even bought a new bathing suit."

"Is that so?" All thoughts of telling Rose about tomorrow fled. He could hardly wait to get to the beach.

Rose tapped her foot to the music. A decent local band played old-time country hits on a small stage in Center Park. Cam's church had also set up a big tent for their annual Fourth of July chicken barbecue complete with corn on the cob and coleslaw.

Other than the tightness of her skin from too much sun at the beach this afternoon, today had been perfect and way more than a simple date. Rose wanted days like today for the rest of her life. She glanced at Cam, still loitering by the dessert table, and her heart squeezed tight inside her chest.

Someone Cam knew stopped to talk to him, delaying the choice of desserts yet again. For a guy who wasn't around much, Cam seemed to know everyone. He'd introduced her to many, boasting about her ability as the new owner of Dean's Hometown Grille even though he'd been the one to make the place shine. Really, the success of the diner had much to do with him—not only his cooking, but his warm smile and welcoming attitude.

"Having fun?" Monica slipped into the chair next to her.

"I am. What about you?" Rose hadn't seen much of Cam's sister all evening. When Monica wasn't working alongside Helen Zelinsky behind the food tables, she'd been talking to a tall man that Rose recognized as the Maple Springs chamber president.

"I suppose, but I do this every year." Monica shrugged. "You look amazing and Cam looks completely smitten. I think we succeeded."

Rose laughed. "I sure hope you're right."

"It's been far too long since he was home for this. I can tell he loves it."

Exactly the kind of words Rose wanted to hear.

Cam returned and set down two plates before her—a slice of cherry pie and a huge brownie. "You choose. Hey, Monica, grab a dessert and join us."

"I'm good." His sister stood. "Besides, I promised Mom I'd help with cleanup."

Rose grabbed hold of Monica's hand and gave it a squeeze. "Thanks, for everything."

Monica gave her a quick hug and whispered, "Good luck."

"What's that all about?" Cam asked.

Rose splayed her fingers. The soft coral polish looked pretty even on her short fingernails. "She went with me to the hair salon and talked me into getting my nails done. See?"

Cam inspected her hands. "That's great. You two seem pretty chummy."

"Yeah, I like your sister a lot." It was nice to have a gal pal.

Cam shrugged. "She's okay. Which dessert do you want?"

Rose gave his shoulder a playful shove. "She's more than okay and you know it. How about we share each dessert?"

"I like sharing with you." Cam offered her the first forkful of pie.

"Yeah?" Rose took a bite without taking her eyes off him.

He smiled. "Yeah."

More of what she wanted to hear. She offered Cam the first bite of brownie. They fed each other, alternating from each plate until Rose busted out laughing.

"What?"

"I feel like a teenager."

He brushed aside her bangs with his fingertips. "Yeah, me, too. Is that so bad?"

"I don't know, maybe. I just turned thirty-one years old." Too old for this giddy feeling.

"A perfect age."

"For what?"

"I'll show you later." Cam made no declarations of his feelings, but the intensity in his eyes and the messages she read there were pretty heady stuff.

Her belly fluttered. She'd never felt like this with Kurt. At eighteen, she didn't know anything about men or relationships. Kurt had swept her off her feet with fairy-tale promises of fame and fortune. Cam didn't promise anything. Her good time hit a speed bump and slowed her down. She'd better rein it in a little.

Rose looked away, out over the bay. The sun sank low in the western sky, casting a luminous golden glow over the water's edge. It wouldn't be dark for a while, but some families had broken out sparklers for their kids. Rose stared at those little sticks of snapping light, praying her plans didn't burn out as quickly and turn to ash.

Rose gasped when tiny white lights strung throughout the trees came on. "Wow. So pretty."

"So are you," Cam whispered.

The band chose that moment to play an older

Randy Travis song. A slow, sweet tune. Dozens of couples popped up and headed for the dance floor.

Cam held out his hand. "Let's dance."

"I was hoping you'd ask."

"You should have said something earlier." He led her onto the already crowded square of parquet flooring set up in front of the band.

"Yes, I should have." Silly, but she'd been afraid of asking Cam to dance. How did she expect to have the guts to ask him to stay in Maple Springs and be her partner? He'd said he liked sharing with her. Would he share his future?

Slipping one arm around her waist, he drew her close. "I've had fun today."

"Me, too." She bolstered her courage. "In fact, I've been thinking…"

He swirled them away from colliding with another couple.

Her breath caught when he pulled her even closer. She swallowed hard. "Uhmmm, Cam—"

"Just dance, Rose." He looped her arms around his neck. "We can talk later."

They moved in lazy circles near the front, swaying to the soft music. She looked into Cam's blue eyes and got lost there. No, not lost, but found. This felt right, as if the one man she'd been meant for had finally been revealed.

He lowered his head and lightly brushed his lips over hers, tentatively, as if asking permission.

Slipping her hand to his chest, she was about to push him back but the thump of his heart matched her own erratic pulse. "We're in the middle of a crowd."

"So?"

She opened her mouth and then closed it, having no good reason or desire to shut down this moment.

He smiled slightly and kissed her again, softly. Ever so slowly he applied more pressure until she finally melted and responded in kind.

The crowd, the music, even the shrieks of children playing with their sparklers faded away. She kissed him back, hoping to convey everything in her heart with touch and taste instead of words. Hoping for so many things.

Cam broke away first and leaned his forehead against hers. "You're amazing."

Now was the time to ask him, so he'd know. "Cam, would you consider staying to run the diner with me, for good?"

His eyes widened. "Rose—"

"We could be partners. You know, once the estate is settled and—"

He laid a finger against her lips. "Let's find a place on the beach for the fireworks, then we can talk."

"Oh. Okay, sure." Rose looked around. Still pretty crowded but some were leaving. No doubt with the same idea. She'd finally said what she wanted, but Cam hadn't reacted the way she'd hoped. Not even close. He didn't look pleased, either. In fact, she'd say he looked trapped.

"Come on." He grabbed her hand and led her to their table, but wouldn't look at her.

A kernel of fear scraped deep in her belly. Rose knew disappointment well and this had every sign of becoming one big fat letdown.

Chapter Twelve

Silently, they gathered up their things but Rose couldn't quiet her thoughts. The earthshaking kiss they had shared didn't match this new tension.

"Bye, Cam and Rose. See you in the morning." Helen Zelinsky waved as she headed to the dance floor with Cam's father.

Rose gathered her wits and waved back. "Are they coming in for breakfast?"

Cam reached for her hand again and pulled her along. "Let's go."

"Cam?" Rose gave him a long look when he didn't answer. She pulled her hand away. "What's the hurry?"

"You'll see in a minute." He turned and crossed the street.

Rose followed.

Once they turned the corner toward the beach, she understood Cam's rush to get there. People were everywhere. A patchwork of blankets already dotted the sand and the grassy park behind them was a maze of chairs and coolers.

"I see a good spot by that big tree." Cam pointed and grabbed her hand once again.

He still hadn't looked her in the eyes. All that heat between them on the dance floor was gone. Even holding Cam's hand, Rose didn't feel the connection anymore. Whatever she was the perfect age for, this certainly wasn't what she'd had in mind.

They walked the length of the beach and Cam finally spread out their blanket half in sand and half on grass in front of a maple tree big enough to lean against.

She plunked down.

He did, too, and gathered up both her hands in his. "Tomorrow morning, I've got an eleven o'clock flight out of Pellston for a meeting with a possible sponsor."

The words were no surprise. "This is what you've been waiting for."

"I've already talked to my mom and she's agreed to help transition the new cook." His voice sounded too serious. Final.

Rose pulled her hands away. "When were you going to tell me?"

"I'm telling you now."

"When did this all come about? Last I knew, you were waiting to hear."

He leaned against the tree trunk with a deep sigh, looking worse than guilty. "Since Friday night. I got a call right before I left your place."

Rose closed her eyes and fought for control, recalling memories of Kurt springing news about gigs and tours on her at the last minute, so she'd have no time to make arrangements to go with him. He'd made decisions that affected her without saying a word, too.

"I should have told you."

She opened her eyes. "Yeah, you should have. You could have called me Friday night. Or yesterday."

"I know, and I'm sorry."

He still hadn't responded to her question about running the diner together, but then, that was a moot point. Rose had her answer. This was the trip he'd waited for and fishing was the career he wanted to return to. She'd known that from the beginning.

How foolish of her to think new hair and some makeup would make him want to stay with her. If this meeting didn't pan out, there'd be others, and Cam would still leave. Time to face facts and put away her pipe dreams. Cam wanted to leave.

"Your mom needn't fill in. I'll be fine."

Cam hated the disappointment in Rose's eyes, knowing he'd put it there. She'd asked him to be her partner at the diner but he couldn't accept. He didn't even know if he wanted to accept. Not now, when he had to see this through and find out what he was really made of.

"I'll be there first thing and make sure they do things right."

"I'm perfectly capable of taking care of a new cook. You don't have to worry about that. Sounds like you're sure of signing." Rose looked at her hands, clasped tightly in her lap.

"Yeah." The date change for the meeting was a good sign they wanted to endorse him.

"I appreciate all you've done, really. Thanks for everything."

"Rose…" He didn't like the finality in her voice and reached for her hands once again. When she didn't pull away, he traced the soft peach color of her painted fingernails, searching for what to say. He'd never been good with words. "I don't want what we've started to end just because I'm going back on the pro fishing circuit. This isn't goodbye."

"Isn't it?" Her eyes filled with tears, but she didn't cry.

Another sucker punch to his gut. "I'll come home between tournaments."

She shook her head. "Long distance doesn't really work for me. Better to stop now before things get serious, you know?"

As far as Cam was concerned, things were already serious between them. "I'm flattered that you'd offer me the chance to help run the diner, but—"

She held up her hand, clearly not interested in hearing him. "I understand."

She didn't.

If he were a better man, he'd explain it so she could. How could he explain that he needed to look in the mirror without this burden of shame? Cam had carried the weight around since he was a kid. He had to make things right before he'd ever hope to get rid of it.

He used to have confidence and the purest love for the sport. So much of that had been stripped away. What good was he if he didn't try to reclaim what he'd lost by his own stupid actions?

"There are some things I need to fix—" Cam's stomach turned. He wanted to leave all that in the past, where it would stay buried, never to happen again. He didn't want Rose to know how low he'd sunk.

The whizzing sound of a small firecracker shot off from the dock of a nearby home caught his attention but didn't quiet his thoughts. This morning's sermon slipped through his mind as if confirming his course, steering him clearly. It was time for him to live his faith with courage. Time to heal some of his own hurts before he could effectively heal hers.

They both watched the green sparkles overhead followed by snaps and crackles that soon fizzled out to nothing. Rose sat composed. She glanced out over the bay waiting for that last strip of twilight to dissolve into darkness like the rest of the crowd. At least she hadn't walked off in a huff.

Sweet, brave Rose wasn't like that.

He wanted to touch her, pull her close and reassure her that they could make it work. After he returned, they'd have more time and he'd do his best to show her that they could make it work.

Cam patted the spot next to him. "There's room for both of us to lean against the tree."

Rose stared at him, as if torn.

He stared back. "Please?"

Finally, she scooted next to him.

The first set of fireworks went off from the barge in the bay. Three at a time exploded overhead, high in the sky with red, white and blue sparks of light.

"It'll be okay, Rose. We'll figure it out." Cam wrapped his arm around her. When she rested her head on his shoulder, he relaxed.

It would be okay. Rose was a keeper and he sure felt like he wanted her for keeps, but he had to redeem his name. It would take work. He wouldn't force his way into her heart until he proved he was worthy of a place there.

The following morning, Rose held her tongue while Cam showed Sheila, the new cook, the prep station, grill and process for filling orders. Hearing the pride in his voice made it hard not to argue her point. He loved doing this, so why wouldn't he stay?

"Thanks for coming in." Rose breathed deep, hoping to dispel the feeling of a lead ball lodged in her chest where her heart should be.

He gave her a searching look. "I'll be back."

"Sure." She wanted to believe him, but what if after he landed the new sponsor he didn't come back?

Greg had shown her the professional fishing schedule of years past online. There were tournaments all over and sponsor commitments at trade shows and events. Cam would be gone more than he'd be home.

Relationships needed time spent together to solidify. Time and care. Two weeks wasn't enough to carry them, and it wasn't as if she could go with Cam, not with a diner to run.

Last night as they'd watched the fireworks together, Rose kept telling herself that Cam wasn't Kurt. Kurt had promised her the sky and delivered thin air. Cam might prove to be very different, if given the chance. She had to give him that chance.

Remembering the feel of his lips on hers, she'd never know if she cut him loose now. Not to mention that Greg looked up to him. Could her son get by with Cam as a distant hero?

"You okay?"

She felt his warm hand cup her elbow. Rose fought the urge to lean into him when his fingers gently caressed the underside of her arm. Looking into his concern-filled gaze wasn't good, either. She knew that he cared, just not enough to stay. Not yet anyway. She had to trust that what they had was not only real, but worth the effort to make last. She couldn't force this.

She forced a smile, though. "I'm fine, and I see a new table of four just came in."

"Let Jess get them. Step in the kitchen with me for a minute."

"What for?"

His blue eyes seemed dimmer and devoid of their usual brilliance. "I don't know. I've got to leave for the airport soon, and I wanted to tell you…"

What else was there to say that couldn't be said when he returned?

"Cam, where's the goat cheese?" Helen searched the prep fridge.

"Go help your mom and Sheila." Rose nodded

toward the door. "I've got orders to take. Call me later, after your meeting, okay?"

"Yeah, sure, okay."

The bell over the door rang, announcing yet more customers coming in. She turned and her stomach dropped and rolled. Kurt's brothers entered the diner and they didn't look like they'd come in for a meal.

Clenching her hands at her sides, Rose smiled wide. "Karl, Kory, can I help you?"

"We received your letter, but do you really think your choices are wise?" Karl sounded so arrogant. And loud.

The noisy level of diner conversations dropped. People listened.

Rose stepped closer to Kurt's brothers. She was in no mood to be intimidated. Keeping her voice low but steady, she said, "This isn't the time to discuss business, but I'll gladly offer you both our special on the house. If you'd like, we can go over everything later this afternoon at your mom's attorney's office."

"I wouldn't eat here if you paid me. And you should be more careful about who you hire." Kory held up a newspaper folded carefully around an inner page article.

Professional Angler Disqualified amid Rumors of Cheating.

Rose stared at that headline and the small picture of Cam that seemed to grow smaller and darker along the edges. She didn't want to believe it, but knew deep down it was true. It was how he'd gotten by in school. Hadn't he said that old habits were hard to break?

She felt Cam's presence close behind her. The tension in him fell like a curtain drawn around her, too, dousing the light. She stepped aside and stared at him.

Cam's features had turned to stone as he snatched the newspaper from Kory. "Where did you get this?"

Helpless, Rose looked around. Customers were openly staring now. Even Jess stood poised with a pitcher of water, watching with wide eyes.

"Let's step in the back, shall we?" Her voice sounded too strong to be her own, but she'd uttered the words.

"We've got nothing to say other than see you in court, Rose Dean." They uttered her last name with contempt, turned and left.

They hadn't been bluffing when they'd first threatened to contest the will. Even if she won, how much cash would they bleed from her in court costs and more attorney's fees?

The chatter of customers had fallen silent. She could hear an old song playing on the country station. "Your Cheatin' Heart" droned on like something out of a nightmare, ringing louder and louder through her head, making it throb.

Rose grabbed the back of a nearby chair before her knees gave out. The Deans' threat reverberated in her ears, too. *See you in court.*

"Rose—"

Divorce papers were court papers. She hated the court.

Once a cheater, always a cheater.

"Is it true?" Her voice sounded harsh now, and raw, as if she'd slipped under ice into the murky depths of frigid water.

Her body shook, too, suddenly freezing in the air-conditioned diner. She knew the answer when he struggled to look her in the eye.

Helen Zelinsky stepped out from behind the counter. "Cam? What's going on?"

"In a minute, Mom."

"Is it?" Rose wanted to hear him tell her that headline was deceptive and false, but knew he couldn't.

He grabbed her arm and walked her to the kitchen. "I can explain."

Hopes smashed again, Rose had heard those words before, too, but the damage had already been done. There was always damage. Fury took hold and pumped hot through her veins, dispelling the cold that had made her tremble.

Rose looked back, over the diner. Jess filled

those plastic tumblers that Cam disliked with water. She heard sounds of scraped plates and chatter filled the air once again, hushed at first but nearly back to normal.

What could he possibly explain? Cam had admitted how he'd stayed under the radar through high school. Even his parents hadn't known how serious his reading issues were because he'd cheated and hid that fact. He'd carried that practice right along into his profession. It wasn't too far a stone's throw to expect he'd cheat on her given the opportunity. He had the smile for it, the flirtatious charm. Her stomach turned. Hadn't she pegged him correctly when she'd first laid eyes on him?

In the kitchen, she shook off Cam's touch. "Cheating's a way of life for you, isn't it?"

"Look, Rose." He let out a deep breath but looked utterly defeated. "Yeah."

"Why?"

"Why does anyone do anything? For the past few years I placed lower and lower in tournaments. One by one, my sponsors starting dropping me. At the time, I didn't see other options."

Rose stared, speechless. It was one thing to cheat in school, he'd only been a kid then, but now? He'd traded his integrity, his very soul, for what? Trophies and prize money.

"Don't look at me like that."

"How do you want me to look?"

"You could try understanding. Our pasts don't dictate our future. I've made some bad mistakes, but I'm trusting that God will show me how to redeem them. Will you give me that chance, too?"

"No." Her mind burned with the memory of how many chances she'd given Kurt.

Patterns formed didn't break easily and Cam had proved that pretty well. Besides, this was not the example she wanted her son to follow. Not by a long shot.

"I wanted to tell you, but feared this kind of reaction."

She sputtered a sarcastic "Oh, really?"

Cam's eyes darkened. "Keeping your heart locked up so tight that there's no room for human frailty is no way to live, Rose. I never meant to hurt you. All this happened before I'd even met you—"

"That's supposed to make it okay?"

"No. That's not what I'm saying—"

"I'd hoped for so much between us—" Her throat threatened to close up on her. "You'd better go, you've got a plane to catch."

"Don't do this." His voice was soft and pleading.

Once a cheater, always a cheater.

She stared him down. She wanted Cam to see

how much this hurt. She wanted him to see what he'd done to her.

Sniffing back tears, she finally said, "Thank you for your help, but I don't need you to come back in the fall. I don't want you to."

Cam looked crushed, but nodded. "For what it's worth, I passed polygraph tests without a hitch. Lies had become truth to me and that was a scary place to be. That was when I knew I needed God. Rose, living in fear steals God's victory in our lives. I know that now. You need to know it, too."

How dare he preach to her! His words rang true even though she didn't want to hear them coming out of his mouth. Hot tears finally tipped and rolled down her cheeks. "Just go, would you? Please."

He did.

Rose heard the bell on the door ring, announcing more customers. She couldn't fall apart yet. Jess waited on too many as it was. She exited the kitchen and hurried past where Cam talked quietly to his mom. She knew Helen would remain the rest of the day and that wasn't going to be easy.

Entering the ladies' restroom, Rose glanced at her reflection in the mirror. Pretty makeup and hair color couldn't hide the hardness in her eyes, the ugliness of broken dreams.

Once again, she'd traded what she knew for what she'd hoped. Shame on her for thinking she could have that fairy tale with Cam. Shame on her for thinking three times was the charm. She'd just struck out.

Cam tossed the newspaper on the metal table that had pots and pans hanging overhead and walked away from Rose. He'd blown it, all right. He'd had the chance to tell her everything about his past last night and didn't take it. Would it have even mattered? Maybe, but not now.

Anger seared his gut. He was mad at the Deans—all of them, especially Kurt for embittering Rose. He was mad at God for letting him lose her, but mostly, he was mad at himself.

"Cam?" His mom called out from the prep station, her face marred with worry. "Don't leave like this, honey."

"I have to."

"No, you don't. You could stay—"

"Trust me, I can't."

His mom didn't look convinced but she gave him a hug anyway. "I love you. Be careful."

"I'll call later." He returned the hug, knowing he'd have to make things right with his parents, too. No more hiding. They deserved the truth, too. All of it.

Scanning the customers sitting on the twirling, vinyl-covered stools at the counter, he knew nearly every one. He'd miss waiting on them and making their orders.

"Where you off to, Cam?" It was one of the elderly guys who liked to fish from the public docks at the waterfront.

To his knowledge, no one around here knew what was in that article. It had been reported last fall by a small-town paper down South where the tournament in question had been held. Cam wasn't such a big name in the sport as to have the story picked up by the major news organizations. Although, he'd seen this same story online along with other sport fishing news. He knew many of his peers had seen it, as well. Rumors had been enough to finally lose his biggest sponsor. No doubt rumors would fly around Maple Springs after today.

Cam Zelinsky is a cheater.

Cam smiled despite the sour taste in his mouth. "Back to fishing, Earl. Take it easy."

"Go get 'em." The old man fist-pumped the air.

"Will do." Cam scanned the diner one last time.

Where was Rose? The thought of her crying somewhere didn't sit well. He'd hurt her more deeply than he'd thought possible, tangled up in what Kurt had done to her. She'd wanted him to run the diner with her and now—

Cam took a deep breath, but the ache inside his chest didn't ease. He would have liked to have said goodbye to Greg, but that would have to keep for now. He'd be back. He'd promised to take the kid ice fishing. It was a promise he intended to keep, if Rose let him.

"Hey, Cam. Whatever's going on, I'm sorry." Jess touched his arm.

"Thanks." He spotted the busboy clearing a table and gave the kid a nod goodbye. "Help her out with the new cook, okay?"

"Of course." Jess shocked him by sniffing back tears.

Cam patted her shoulder. There wasn't much he could say.

He checked his watch. Time to go or he'd be late, but he couldn't seem to make his feet move. He spotted Rose as she exited the bathroom and her gaze slammed into his. She didn't look fragile or weepy, but hard. Disgusted.

Whatever chances he might have had with her were gone. Looking into her pretty green eyes, he clearly read the message there. It was over. They were through.

Chapter Thirteen

Rose finally locked the doors of the diner and leaned against the glass with a shudder. She'd made it through until close without coming unglued. In less than an hour, she'd be free to have a good cry. Hopefully, before Greg came home.

What was she going to tell Greg?

Rose watched Helen help Sheila clean up, stacking food on the silver cart Cam had always used, and those pesky tears threatened. She'd fought them all afternoon. Cam's mom had made it worse with her sympathetic glances and reassuring touches.

Helen refused to skip out, even after Rose had told her she'd take care of cleanup with the new cook. Helen wouldn't hear of it and Rose wasn't sure if the woman did all this out of guilt over what her son had done or genuine affection. Maybe a little of both.

When everything was done, the new cook gave her puppy-eyed looks, too. "I'll see you tomorrow."

"Thanks, Sheila." They'd do all right.

"Did Cam tell you this wasn't true?" Helen lay the newspaper article on the counter.

Rose shook her head. Oh, how she wished that had been the case. Cam's deceit ran so deep that he'd believed it as truth. How could that happen?

His mother sighed. "I knew something was wrong when he'd been so miserable this past winter. That kid can smile his way through anything, but not this time. He'd told us he'd lost his last sponsor because of low placements and then the issue about practicing where he shouldn't have during a tournament. Of all my kids, Cam's the most private. He doesn't open up."

He'd opened up with her, but only to a point. Rose saw the distress in Helen's eyes and her heart twisted anew. They were both moms with sons. This was hard on Helen, too. "I'm sorry."

"Rose, I know you're upset but Cam—"

Rose's cell phone rang, interrupting whatever Helen was about to say. The number belonged to her attorney. Linda's attorney. "Hello? Can you hang on a moment?"

Rose looked at Helen. "I have to take this."

Helen gently brushed her back. "Call me tonight if you need to talk. Cam loves you, Rose.

Please, give him a second chance. He's not the same man as before. I can see it."

Would you believe that I made a deal with God?

Cam had said that the first day she'd met him. She'd believed it, too. Tears threatened again at the compassion in Helen's eyes. The words she offered were sweet, but Rose couldn't risk it. She'd read the article in its entirety. Other fishermen who'd been proven cheaters had faced huge fines and some had even gone to jail.

Cam may have invited God into his heart, she didn't doubt that, but when push came to shove, what would he do? When the pressure was high, would Cam rely on the Lord or slip back into old habits or worse?

Rose couldn't take that chance. She couldn't go through divorce papers again. "Thanks, but I— Thanks."

Helen gave her shoulder a squeeze and left.

Rose drew in a sustaining breath. She had a diner to keep and hopefully Linda's attorney had some news. "Sorry about that."

"I heard you were paid a little visit from Linda's sons."

Wow, news traveled fast. "Who told you?"

"Does it matter? Listen, that's harassment plain and simple and I think we should throw down a threat of our own with an order to cease and desist or we'll sue for harassment."

Rose's mind whirled right along with her stomach. More fees and court papers. "Won't that make them even angrier?"

"We're not only calling their bluff, but laying the groundwork for our case if they ever follow through on contesting."

Rose was done lying down and taking it. This was her diner, Greg's legacy, and she'd fight to keep it. "Okay, do it."

Rose heard Helen leave through the back door. She heard more noises in the kitchen and wondered if Helen had forgotten something, but then Greg entered with a tall glass of milk in hand. A real glass. Another reminder of Cam pinched her heart.

Cam had brought those glasses in for his iced tea. He'd said that he couldn't do plastic and ventured to guess the customers thought the same thing. Rose had laughed at him. She wasn't about to switch from plastic to glass. It was too expensive and real glasses broke too easily.

Everything in her life seemed to break easily.

Rose hadn't expected Greg home quite this soon, but waved him in. "How was it?"

"Great." Greg looked at her, confused. "Where's Cam?"

How was she going to explain this one? "He's gone, Greg. He had a meeting with a sponsor and won't be back—"

"Who's going to cook?"

"You know that Cam and I had interviewed cooks so he could go back to fishing. He went back."

"But that's not till August." Her son lifted the lid of the acrylic baked-good case and reached for a cookie. His attention zeroed in on the newspaper she'd left lying there, the article about Cam still faceup. Greg grabbed it. "What's this?"

Rose darted to snatch it away, but it was too late. Helpless, she watched the color drain from her son's face as he read the headline. "Greg—"

He pinned her with accusing eyes. "You made him leave, didn't you?"

"I didn't make him leave. He had a meeting—"

"You hired a new cook and said he's not coming back. I didn't even get to say goodbye." Her son's voice grew shrill.

She touched his arm. "Listen to me—"

"No. You listen." He pulled away from her. "You always make them leave. You made Cam leave just like you did Dad!"

She sucked in air, but couldn't seem to breathe. "Greg…"

"Leave me alone." He threw the paper down and shoved hard off the stool, tipping over his glass of milk. It rolled and fell to the floor, smashing as it hit.

"Greg!"

He dashed for the front door, unlocked it, threw it open and ran outside.

Rose let him go. She stared at the spilled milk dripping onto the floor where shards of broken glass lay in a white puddle. That was why she didn't want real glasses in her diner. Her body shook as tears seared her cheeks.

"Why'd You bring me here only to ruin everything?" Leaning against the counter, she wailed against God.

There was no answer. Only drops of milk hitting the floor.

Rose slipped onto a stool, hung her head and wept.

Cam paced his hotel room. His meeting had gone great, but he found little joy in gaining a huge sponsor. He couldn't share his news with the one person whose opinion mattered more than any other. It was too late to call Rose and he doubted she'd talk to him anyway.

He hated the way they'd parted. He hated that she'd seen that article. Hated it even more that it was all true. It didn't matter that there hadn't been any proof found to substantiate the rumors. It didn't matter that he'd been disqualified from that tournament for a breach of practice rules. He'd cheated, plain and simple. It hadn't been the first time, but he vowed it would be the last.

God had offered up the chance to prove he could do it, too, and provided the financial backing for next year. An iced tea company had signed him, as well, and his business manager said there would be more.

The electronics giant wanted him to attend an outdoor expo this upcoming weekend as a spokesperson for their GPS mapping and sonar imaging products. There was no point in going home. Not yet anyway.

He grabbed his cell phone and called his mom to let her know his change in plans.

"Cam?" His mom's voice sounded fuzzy.

"I'm sorry, did I wake you?" He glanced at his watch. It was after ten.

"It's okay. What happened?"

"I have a couple of sponsors with more on the radar. I'm working a nearby outdoor expo this weekend in Kansas City, so I won't be home for a bit. How'd the new cook do?"

His mom sighed. *"She's fine. She'll be good. Cam, Rose is really torn up. Why would you do such a thing?"*

An image of Rose crying turned him inside out. "I've made mistakes, Mom. Mistakes that I'm trying to fix."

"Where does that leave Rose? Monica said that she wanted you to stay and run the diner with her."

Why did his sister have to tell? He'd burned

that bridge. He'd never forget the look in Rose's eyes, as if he'd become some monster right in front of her.

"I'm pretty sure she doesn't want that anymore. Look, Mom, the Deans are threatening to contest Linda's will unless Rose sells them back the diner."

At his mother's sharp intake of breath, he added, "Keep an eye on her for me. I've got my manager checking some legal channels, but there's little I can do. Make sure she and Greg are okay. Make them dinner or something. Rose can't really cook."

"Already ahead of you. Monica took over lasagna tonight."

"Thanks, Mom. If you see Greg…" Cam ran a hand through his hair. Would Rose let him see the kid again? His gut turned. "If you see Greg, tell him… I don't know what to tell him."

"When the time's right, you will tell him yourself. Don't worry, we'll stick close to Rose."

Picking up the pieces of the mess he'd made. Cam's throat thickened. "Thanks, Mom. Got to go."

He didn't wait for her goodbye and ended the call. Hanging his head in his hands, Cam prayed. Hard. He asked God to comfort Rose and speak to her heart, but his phone buzzed with an incoming call, interrupting his pleas.

When he saw that the number belonged to Rose, his heart leaped. "Hello?"

"Cam?" Greg had his mom's phone.

"What's up, bud?"

The kid was quiet for a few seconds. *"I, um, just wanted to call."*

Cam sighed. "Where's your mom?"

"She's sleeping."

So, Rose didn't know about this. Cam needed to tread lightly. He certainly didn't want to make things worse. "Everything okay, Greg?"

"Did you leave because of that story in the paper?"

Cam closed his eyes. The kid had seen it then. If Rose had shown it to her son, that was a really low blow. She wanted nothing more to do with him, but did she have to ruin Greg's view of him, too? "I had a meeting with a new sponsor, plus I have some expos I have to attend."

"Why'd they say that stuff about you?"

Cam's gut turned. Could he use this as one of those teachable moments with Greg? Show the kid what not to do? But how would he ever know if he'd handled it right if he wasn't around enough to find out?

Taking a deep breath, Cam wasn't sure where to start, but he was done ducking the truth. "Because I've made some really bad choices, Greg. My whole life, I've done things that were wrong, and I can't just take it all back. I wish I could, but I can't. I let my family down, your mom. Even you. And I'm sorry. God's forgiven me but He's also given me the chance to make some things right again."

"Aren't you coming back?" The kid's voice sounded watery.

"Not for a while."

"What about my mom? Do you still like her?"

"I love your mom—" That rolled off his tongue so easily.

He loved Rose.

It wasn't the love-thy-neighbor kind of love, either, even if that was what he'd meant to convey to the kid. "I love you, too, bud, but we knew I'd be going back to fishing. This time, I need to do it the right way, understand?"

"Yeah."

When the kid sniffed, Cam's heart broke. "It's late, Greg. I got to go, buddy. Listen to your mom, okay? This isn't easy on her."

Another sniff.

"You okay?"

"I wish you didn't leave."

"I'll be back. Don't forget, we've got more fishing to do." Cam hoped that might still happen.

"Yeah, okay. Bye, Cam." Greg didn't sound like he believed him. Why should he?

"Bye, bud." He disconnected with an even heavier heart.

That kid needed him. Cam's past had messed with his chances to be there for the boy. Cam wanted to watch him grow up and help him navigate those rough teenaged waters.

Rubbing the back of his neck, Cam wondered for the umpteenth time if returning to the pro fishing circuit was the right thing to do. What if all this was about his own pride? If he'd stayed, he might have helped Rose fight the Deans. He could have stood by her, been the kind of man she needed. The kind of man she deserved.

But after that article had been flashed in her face, the end result might still have been the same. He'd lost the fragile trust Rose might have had in him and there was only one way to win it back. He had to prove that he was different than before. A better man. A man she could trust.

Cam grabbed the hotel Bible from the top drawer of the nightstand. For one thing, God was real to him now. Opening the pages, he used the exercises Rose had showed him. He'd been plodding through those workbooks, but the words still jumped around on the page, some even upside down. He snapped the book shut. If he was ever going to make something of himself, he needed to read better.

Opening the internet browser on his phone, Cam looked up those classes Rose had told him about. There happened to be a facilitator in western Missouri, maybe an hour or so away. He saved the number in his contacts list and made a mental note to call tomorrow.

He loved Rose and he wanted her back, but he had to prove to her that he was worth taking back.

The following afternoon, Rose stared at the computer screen ablaze with photos of professional bass fishermen. She'd read the article, but wanted to dig up every tidbit of information she could on Cam before Greg got home. Twisted, maybe, but she had to know more. Too bad she hadn't done this after they'd first met. She might have kept her distance a little better and protected her heart. Greg's, too.

Today had been agony, with reminders of Cam everywhere. If it wasn't her new cook at the grill doing things differently, it was every person she'd waited on asking where Cam was. She'd responded cheerily enough about his return to fishing, but the fake smile she'd worn all day made her face hurt. Remorse made her heart ache. She was sorry she'd met Cam, sorry she'd reinvented herself for him when he hadn't been worth the effort.

Rose closed her eyes tight.

That wasn't quite true or fair. She'd crawled into looking plain in order to hide. Since meeting Cam, she'd felt more alive than she had in years. He had brought her back to who she'd once been, before all the hurts and disappointments ate away at her confidence.

They were both hiding. Afraid of so many things.

Fighting the quicksand of self-pity, Rose turned to prayer and begged God to show her what lay ahead. How many times had she prayed this very prayer, knowing those answers wouldn't come? God wasn't a crystal ball. He was a lamp unto her feet that shone only so far. Lately, only a few forward steps.

God wanted her trust and her dependence.

Her forgiveness.

She sucked in a sob when those words whispered through her thoughts. *No.* How many times must she forgive being left and lied to?

Seventy times seven.

Rose shook her head against that snip of scripture that came to mind. Some things were just too hard.

Her phone rang. Checking the number, she picked up, grateful for something else to focus on. Her lawyer had express mailed a letter requesting the Deans stop harassing her or face a legal action. There was nothing more she could do but wait it out.

That placed her right back where she'd started. Linda's estate should be closed in the next couple of months. Any contesting after that would be a moot point.

Rose thanked him and disconnected. Glancing at her recent call list, Rose noticed a phone call made last night, after she'd gone to bed. Her breath caught when she recognized the cell number as Cam's. She heard footsteps coming up the steps and glanced at the door.

"Hey, Mom." Greg entered the apartment.

"Did you call Cam?"

Her son took a belligerent stance, ready for her to make something of it. "Yeah."

"Oh, Greg, why?"

"I didn't get to say goodbye. You made him leave before I got home."

Rose sighed. It didn't matter that Cam had had a plane to catch; Greg was still mad at her. How this was her fault, she couldn't figure.

Her son went to the fridge and opened it. "He's got a sponsor now, so he's not coming home."

"I see." Rose's spirit sank lower.

She'd sort of hoped that his meeting would fail so he'd have to come home, but then, she'd given him no reason to return for her. Maybe that was for the best.

"He loves you, Mom." Greg carried a gallon of milk in one hand and a plate of leftover lasagna from Helen in the other. He set everything on the counter, then grabbed a glass from the cupboard overhead.

"Where would you get that idea?"

"He told me." Her son popped the plate in the microwave and hit Start, then clicked on the radio. Contemporary Christian music poured out, competing with the whir of the microwave.

Rose sat as if struck, until fire seeped through her. "He had no business telling you that!"

Greg looked surprised by her sharp tone. "He said he was sorry for what he did."

Using her son that way... Rose fumed. "No more calls to Cam, you got me?"

"You can't do that!"

She could and would. "I mean it, Greg."

Her son glared at her. "He's my friend, too, and he promised to take me ice fishing."

"That's months away."

"So?"

"So..." Rose searched for reasons that didn't come.

She wanted to yell back that Cam wasn't a good example of what a man should be. He was no role model, but images of Cam and his family taking Greg under their wings to play horseshoes and fishing flashed through her mind. Greg looked up to Cam, even seeking out his counsel instead of hers regarding last weekend's camping trip. Cam had been so proud of Greg catching fish...

That seemed like eons ago.

The microwave beeped.

Monica had brought over a huge pan of lasagna that Helen had made for them. They cared about her and Greg. Truly cared.

Silence settled like a thick blanket, heavy and dragging her down.

I've made mistakes, bad ones.

Cam's words smote her, but the defeat in his eyes when he'd said them had haunted her all night long. Should she really be casting these stones?

The song playing on the radio in the background suddenly seemed louder and sounded so familiar. She realized it was the same tune that Cam had often hummed while he worked.

Listening to the words about grace and mercy and sin being washed white by Jesus's blood at the Cross, Rose was humbled. What if God had withheld His forgiveness from her? Where would she be?

Tears filled her eyes and she ground them away with the heels of her palms. She refused to cry in front of her son, but it didn't look like she had much of a choice. She couldn't hold them back.

"Don't cry, Mom."

She felt his hands on her shoulders and whispered, "I'm trying to protect both of us. Don't you see?"

"Sometimes you have to take a chance. That's

what you told me about moving here." Her boy, so young and yet wise for his soon-to-be twelve years, wrapped his arms around her. "It'll be okay, Mom. You'll see."

Rose twisted in her chair so she could hug her son. She held on tightly while more of the words of the song washed over her. Hope and holy ground. All she need do is surrender.

God had blessed her with such a good boy. Greg was growing into a strong young teen she could be proud of. Her heart nearly burst when she thought about it—Greg had challenged her lack of faith and helped her to see.

Rose needed to trust in the Lord like never before. Trust that the diner would truly be hers to keep and trust that it would be okay. Maybe her son knew something she refused to consider. Cam wasn't Kurt. Cam was Cam, and if she truly loved him, she needed to release whatever happened with him into God's capable hands and trust that He knew best. God certainly knew her heart's desire. Cam did, as well.

Giving her son a squeeze before letting go, she whispered, "Thanks, Greg. I needed to hear that, and I'm going to hope and trust that you're right."

"'Course I am." Her son smiled, looking so much like his father, but Greg had sounded exactly like Cam.

Chapter Fourteen

Cam crossed a busy Main Street. The summer crowd remained in full swing and would be for another month yet. Cloudy days brought out shoppers and tourists that clogged up the sidewalks. Parking spots were coveted. He'd seen several folks drive slowly, looking for openings that weren't there, only to circle round again. He knew how it felt. Right now, he felt like those people in their cars, circling in hopes of finding rest and a place to park it for good.

It had been three weeks since he'd last been home. Three weeks since he'd left the diner, feeling as if a rug had been pulled out from under him. Three long weeks shouldn't have fazed him, he'd traveled constantly for most of his adult life, but this time away had been tough on many levels.

Rose had surprised him by calling just a little while ago. She'd asked if he'd meet her at the beach today if he wasn't busy. He'd asked why the waterfront instead of the diner, but Rose hadn't answered. That didn't bode well and he hoped to God the Deans hadn't ripped that place away from her.

He spotted her on the beach and his stomach tightened. She looked prettier than ever holding her sandals in one hand and swishing her feet in the water.

Her worried gaze slammed into his.

He waved.

She waved back with the slightest of smiles.

When he finally reached her, Cam buried his hands in his pockets to keep from touching her. "Hey."

Rose smoothed her super-blond hair. "How are you?"

"I'm good." He had so much to tell her, but that would have to keep until he knew why she'd wanted to meet. "How about you? How's the diner?"

She shrugged. "It's okay. Sheila's doing a good job."

"Better than me?" He couldn't help it and had to tease.

Rose gave him a real smile then. "No, not better than you."

"Good." He breathed easier. "The Deans still bothering you?"

"Haven't heard a word since…" She looked down at her feet.

Since *that* day.

"We're all managing just fine."

Without him.

"Good." Never one with words, he was at a loss what to say next. He'd missed her, but didn't think she'd welcome hearing about it. Rose seemed distant, wary.

"Maybe we can sit?" She gestured toward a bench not far from the water.

"Sure." He sat down after she did, keeping a polite distance between them. He looked out over Maple Bay where a gray sky met calm gray waters. There wasn't a breeze, which was too bad; a slight chop would make it perfect for fishing.

The wooden bench creaked when Rose turned toward him. "Cam, I wanted to apologize for the way I reacted after seeing that article."

He blinked and his pulse kicked up a beat or two. This was a nice way to start. "I wish it would have come from me instead of you finding out the way you did. For that, I'm truly sorry. It's not something I'm proud of. Not at all."

"I know." She looked down at her hands folded in her lap. "I asked Greg not to call you again, until after I spoke with you and made sure you didn't mind. I didn't want to do that over the phone and since Monica told me that you'd come home last night, I called."

"I had to get my gear. I'm heading for Virginia next week."

"That's right. Greg's looking forward to following your progress."

His hopes that maybe they could regroup and move forward sunk. "So, this is about Greg?"

She looked up, alarmed. "He wants to talk to you, see you before you go, but I don't want him hurt, not if you're busy and would rather not be bothered."

"Is that why you chose to meet here, so I wouldn't run into your son at the diner? Did you think I'd taken an interest in Greg only to get to you?"

"I—" Her eyes widened at his sharp tone and her mouth fell open. "Well, yeah, maybe. It's happened before."

She'd lumped him in with those other men in her life and he couldn't say he blamed her. He hadn't been truthful with her when he'd had the opportunity. Something he'd always regret.

They fell silent and he glanced at her luscious mouth, remembering the feel of her lips against his as if he'd just tasted them.

He couldn't stand this. "Rose, I love Greg. He's a good kid and I'd like to help where I can. And I love you."

She closed her eyes. "Please don't."

"I know you're scared. I am, too."

Her eyes looked bright and shiny when she opened them. "You're right, I am scared. I'm scared of making the same mistakes I made with Greg's father. My son looks up to you, Cam, he needs you, but I won't ruin that for him by throwing caution to the wind when it comes to my needs."

"I'm not Kurt."

"I know that but—"

He brushed back her bangs with his fingers until she looked at him. "Rose, I'm not Kurt."

Her eyes filled with tears. "It's hard to let all that go."

He imagined it must be and words were inadequate, but he'd try. "Now, more than ever, I need to honor God with my fishing. He gave me a second chance and I have to take it."

"I understand. Really, I do." Rose still looked hurt, though. And skeptical.

"You don't trust me to do it right, do you?" He wished she'd never seen that article.

"Cam—" She blew out her breath, but didn't continue.

He couldn't blame her for doubting him. What proof did she have that he'd changed? Nothing yet. He had to prove he was worthy not only of her trust, but everyone else's, too. Things were different now. They had to be.

Seeing her, though, made him want to take the easy route and rush things along. He wanted her to be his without the prep work that lay before him. Always looking for shortcuts, Cam might battle the tendency to cut corners for the rest of his life. A future with Rose was bigger than any tournament he'd ever fish and he'd do his part to get there the right way.

Starting now. Instead of arguing his case, he simply took her hand and listened. "Go on."

She gave his hand a squeeze before pulling away. "I forgive you, really, I do, and I know all that is in the past, but I still need to guard my future. It's not like we won't ever talk again, I just— I'd like you to be there for Greg, if you're willing."

That spoke volumes. She trusted him with her son. "I am willing. I'd be glad to talk to Greg anytime he needs it. I'm here for a couple days, maybe I can take him fishing."

Rose nodded. "He'd love that."

"What about you, Rose? What would you love?"

She looked him square in the eye. "You already know the answer to that."

He did know, and boy was he grateful it was still true. He had a chance. *They* had a chance. One day, there'd be no stopping him from earning the prize of Rose's heart.

* * *

The passing of Labor Day announced the end of summer and the beginning of a new school year. It also brought new challenges for Rose. Sheila, her cook, gave her notice to leave for culinary classes by the end of September. Rose had placed an ad, but it really didn't matter who she hired. No one could replace Cam with his wild-colored bandannas and ardent smiles. He'd been the pulse of this diner, making everything beat with vibrant warmth.

He'd been the pulse in her, too, bringing her back to life. She missed him more than ever and looked forward to seeing him again when he came home from a tournament in Tennessee. Picking up where they'd left off was another matter, though. She was still afraid of the long distances that came with loving Cam. The what-might-happens still had a hold on her.

Even with Greg back at school, he and his friend Jeff still fished the waterfront nearly every day. Rain or shine, they were out there casting from the public docks. Greg used the fishing tackle that Cam had given him, as well as some new lures Cam had sent for Greg's birthday. He hadn't forgotten the date, which was more than could be said for Kurt.

A couple of times, Greg brought home fish he'd caught and couldn't wait to tell Cam. Jeff's dad had cleaned them, but Greg cooked them. He'd learned how to fry fish from his camping trip but learned how to broil it from Cam's instructions over the phone.

The two spoke a couple times a week. Listening to them compare fishing notes, Rose felt adrift navigating these waters alone. She spoke to Cam, as well, but she purposefully kept it short and friendly. She hadn't for a moment forgotten the words he'd told her when they sat on that bench over a month ago.

Cam had said that he loved her and she longed to believe him, yet once he qualified for next year's professional series, he'd be home even less. She'd seen the fishing schedules online and Southern tournaments started in January.

Greg followed Cam's progress online, too. He'd placed well in the earlier two of three regional open tournaments. Her son had explained that Cam needed the cumulative points from all three regional opens to place him in the top five in order for him to even qualify for next year's pro series. That one more tournament to finish had started two days ago.

Part of her wanted him to lose, even though it wasn't right to wish defeat on anyone. She wished Cam wanted what she wanted, but she didn't want it by some default of circumstance. Cam needed a win.

Her waitress waved as she left. "Bye, Rose. Have a good weekend."

"You, too, Jess." Rose locked up the diner and peered out the large window overlooking Main.

It had been a cold and dreary Saturday. A good day for a nap, which she planned to take now that she'd closed up shop. Through rivulets of rain running down the glass, she noticed the maple trees across the street had started to turn. Patches of gold and peachy-orange leaves fluttered at the top. It wouldn't be long before the whole tree blazed with fall color.

Time to head upstairs with the leftover tomato basil soup from today's special, which had been paired with grilled cheese. It was good, but Cam would have made something with more pizzazz. He'd promised to teach her how to cook, but that had been cut short. Her decision, not his.

The thought of spending an evening with him, cuddled up in front of the fireplace at his house, sliced sharp with longing. She'd been smart to stall things between them. If she missed him this badly, it would have been worse had they been truly serious.

She let her forehead rest against the cold glass of her front door and sighed. Who was she trying to kid? In spite of everything, she still loved him. Her feelings for Cam had neither changed nor lessened. Maybe she hadn't been so smart after all.

She grabbed the leftover pot of soup and headed upstairs, where Greg watched a baseball game on TV.

"What's that?"

"Tomato soup. Want some? I can make grilled cheese to go with it." She could handle a basic grilled cheese sandwich.

"Sure."

Rose went about fixing lunch for herself and Greg. When they were both seated with food in front of them and prayers said, Rose tipped her head. "No fishing this afternoon?"

"Nope. I don't want to miss Cam's final weigh-in. It'll be live online in a couple hours."

"Ah."

Greg had watched the last two days' worth of results on the computer. Cam had done well, but had stayed just north of the middle of the pack. Seeing him smile, seeing him bleached and browned from the sun, even online, made her heart ache.

When they were finished eating, Rose put the soup in the fridge. "I'm going to lie on your bed and read."

"Okay, sure, Mom."

She tucked herself under the covers and cracked open a book she'd been reading. She hadn't made it further than a few pages when her eyelids grew heavy.

"Mom! Mom, come here!"

Rose awoke with a start. She blinked and heard her son's call again.

"Mom, you've got to see this." He stood in the bedroom's entrance now, his face flushed with excitement. "Come on, hurry."

Rose sat up and yawned. Still daylight outside, but only barely. "What is it?"

Greg grinned. "Come and see."

She followed her son into the living room.

He pulled out the chair at the computer desk for her and hit the play button on-screen. "Watch this."

Rose watched a video clip of an interview with Cam. He hadn't won, but came in a close second. When asked about his comeback from disqualification, Cam glowed as he gave all the credit to God, who had not only redeemed his soul, but had given him a chance to redeem his career and end it on a high note. An honest one, he said.

Rose felt her stomach flip. *End?*

Cam proceeded to tell the announcer that he was stepping down from professional fishing.

"What are you going to do?" the man asked.

Cam looked right into the camera. "That all depends on one very special lady."

Rose gasped and covered her mouth. Cam had quit his fishing career for her? To be with her and Greg? He didn't look sorry about it, either. Cam looked happy.

"Maybe now you'll believe that he really loves you, Mom."

Greg seemed far too grown-up for a boy who'd recently turned twelve.

Rose looked at her son and smiled. This time she didn't wipe away the tears streaming down her face. Speechless, all she could do was laugh.

Greg did, too, until her cell phone rang and her son handed it to her.

It couldn't be Cam. Scanning the screen, Rose saw that it was his mother. Helen called to see if Rose had seen Cam online. More tears of joy and when Rose finally disconnected, she looked at Greg.

"You going to call him?"

Rose nodded. "A little later, though, don't you think? I mean, what if he's still at the weigh-in?"

"So?"

"So…" Rose bit her lip.

"Call him, Mom." Then her son left for his room, giving her privacy.

Rose glanced at the computer screen. Greg had hit Pause after Cam's interview was over, but the image of him with his arms raised in triumph remained. She ran her finger over the screen and whispered, "I promise you won't regret this."

Rose tapped Cam's name in her contacts and waited. Her heart hammered in her chest. She'd leave a message if she had to.

"Hey." His voice sounded soft amid the rowdy sounds surrounding him.

"I saw it, Cam. I saw you just now. Greg and I watched your interview. I—" Emotion stuck in her throat, cutting off her words.

"I'm coming home, Rose. For good." More noise.

She needed to let him go so he could celebrate his last tournament. "I'll be waiting. And Cam?"

"Yeah?"

"I love you." She could hear him breathe in and could easily imagine a smile spreading across his handsome face. That was enough for now. "See you soon."

"Tomorrow, Rose. I'll be home tomorrow." He disconnected.

She closed her eyes and whispered her thanks to God. Then she replayed Cam's interview again to make sure she hadn't been dreaming.

Cam entered the diner through the back door. He still had his key. After arriving home in the early-morning hours, Cam had grabbed a few hours of sleep while Rose was at church. He'd showered before calling her moments ago to say he was on his way. At the foot of the stairs, he heard the door open above, and Rose stepped out.

He set down the gift bags he'd brought and smiled. "Hey."

She raced down the steps and launched herself into his arms. "I missed you so much. It never got better, the missing you."

"I know." He held her close and breathed in her scent. Sweet and flowery and still dangerous.

She pulled back, looking amazed. "I thought you'd planned to fish next year if you qualified."

He was pretty amazed, too. "That was the plan."

"Then what—"

Cam ran his lips lightly over hers. "I just didn't want to do it anymore." Never before had he been this certain of a decision. He looked up the stairs and spotted Greg waiting above.

He waved the kid down. "Come here, buddy."

"That was awesome, online." Greg tromped down the stairs.

Rose shifted to pull away, but Cam didn't let her go. He made room for Greg and embraced them both. "It's good to be home."

"Come upstairs. Have you had lunch? I've got tomato soup left over from yesterday."

"We're going out to celebrate. The three of us." Cam grabbed the gift bags and followed Rose up the steps to her apartment.

Greg zeroed in on those bags. "Are those for us?"

"Greg!" Rose scolded.

Cam chuckled and handed the boy the larger of the two. "This one's for you."

"Iced tea?" Rose started for the kitchenette.

Cam stopped her by circling his arm around her waist. "I'm fine. Stay here, okay? I have something to give you, too."

"Wow, Cam. Thanks." Greg pulled out a black parka with a matching pair of bib overalls and waterproof gloves.

Rose shook her head. That gear must have cost a mint.

"For ice fishing," Cam said.

Rose smiled. "I figured as much."

"Is that one for Mom?" Greg pointed to the small bag.

Cam handed it over. "It is."

Rose looked inside and pulled out a book. *The Swiss Family Robinson* copy she'd lent him.

"I read it, Rose. Start to finish. And two more books, as well."

Her eyes filled with tears but he could read the pride there. Pride in him. "When?"

"I found one of those classes you and Greg took, so I enrolled. It was one of the toughest weeks of my life, but worth it. I'm going to do a follow-up downstate. Look inside the cover."

One tear escaped. Running down her cheek, it fell on the fifteen-thousand-dollar check he'd signed over to her and placed inside. She sucked in a breath and then stared at him. Hard. "Your prize money?"

He grinned. "If your offer still stands, that's my first installment toward buying into the diner. It can go toward legal fees if the Deans go through with their threat to contest. Either way, I want to help you fight them. I want to be your partner, Rose."

"Of course the offer still stands." She jumped up, grabbed a folder from the desk behind them and handed it to him. "But there's no need to fight. Look at this."

Aloud, he read the letter from her attorney, Linda's lawyer, announcing that the estate had been closed. He glanced at her, proud that he'd read it without once stumbling.

She gave him the brightest smile he'd ever seen. It lit up her face and shone right through to his heart. "Keep looking," she told him.

He was done looking—done hiding, too. He wanted Rose and everything that came with her. He'd planned on asking her privately, after discussing his proposal with her son, but he didn't think he could wait for all that. Maybe this once, taking a shortcut would be okay.

She pointed at the copy of a filed deed to the building that had been transferred into Rose's name. "It's mine, Cam. The Deans never followed through on their threat. Now it can be ours."

He glanced at Greg.

The kid nodded as if he knew. Of course he did. Greg would have to be blind not to see how he felt.

Cam set the papers aside, then got down on one knee. He cleared his throat and reached for her hand. "Marry me, Rose. If you and Greg are willing, let's partner for life and be a family."

Rose smiled and reached for her son. "What do you think, Greg?"

"I think you should say yes." Greg's voice sounded thick.

"I think so, too." Rose said simply, "Yes."

"I love you guys." Cam gathered both of them in his arms for an embrace that promised a lifetime of togetherness. He wasn't going to miss another moment and that felt good. Better than he'd ever expected.

Greg pulled away with a sniff. "I'm going to try on my ice fishing gear."

Cam nodded. "Thanks for saying yes, bud."

The kid gave him a watery smile as he gathered up the bibs and jacket and headed for his room.

Rose stayed put, on her knees next to him. "I think we should change the name of the diner, though."

"To what?" He rubbed his nose against hers.

"Drop the 'Dean's,' but I'm not adding 'Zelinsky.'"

Cam laughed. "Hometown Grille. I like the sound of that."

"Me, too. Welcome home, Cam." Then Rose kissed him, deeply and thoroughly.

Cam had never felt so complete. Pulling back, he smiled. "It's good to be home."

Epilogue

It might have been a cold Saturday in November to get married but Rose thought it was perfect. Also, the perfect time to close up the diner for the week of Thanksgiving while she and Cam went on their honeymoon in the Florida Keys.

She and Greg had moved their things into Cam's house and her parents were staying there to watch Greg while she and Cam were away. Helen had a huge Thanksgiving meal planned for all of them, making Rose almost sorry they'd miss it. Almost. They had reservations tonight at a posh hotel before flying out in the morning. There'd be plenty more family Thanksgivings to come.

Her gown swished as she walked toward her father, waiting for her at the double-door entrance to the sanctuary. Rose had so much to be thankful for.

"Oh, Rose, you look beautiful." He offered his arm. "Ready?"

"In a minute." She shifted her bouquet of deep orange roses, then looped her hand into the crook of his elbow but didn't move, not yet. Having never before walked down the aisle in a church, Rose wanted to savor the moment.

She wore her mother's ivory silk and lace wedding dress with only minor alterations. The poofs had been taken out of the long sleeves and the train had been removed so the entire skirt swirled above her feet. With Monica's help, Rose had found a pair of kid leather ivory ankle boots with ribbon laces to match.

She scanned the pews filled with Cam's family and hers. Their faces all turned toward her, waiting. She spotted her mom looking radiantly happy. Rose couldn't help but blow her a kiss.

She'd honored her parents' wish for a church wedding followed by a catered lunch reception in the fellowship hall downstairs. Spotting the cored-out pumpkin vases stuffed with deep orange roses, berries and mini cattails that lined the front pews, Rose felt part of an even bigger family. She'd had a blast arranging her own flowers with the help of her mom, along with Helen and Cam's sisters. Larger pumpkins with more of the same flowers graced the altar.

The minister from the congregation where Rose had grown up stood beside the pastor of this small community church that she and Cam now called home. In front of them, Greg stood dressed in a fine dark gray suit. He smiled at her, looking proud and far older than his tender years. Rose blew him a kiss, too, and nearly laughed when her son rolled his eyes.

Then she gazed at Cam and nearly lost it. He grinned, but his brilliant blue eyes looked shiny with barely controlled emotion. *Love.* He truly loved her. She couldn't wait to join him there at the altar and for the rest of their lives.

Rose took a deep breath and squeezed her dad's arm. "Okay, I'm ready."

The music changed to the song Cam had hummed so many times at the diner. It was their song, this song about the Cross. A testament to the amazing power of God's grace and forgiveness in their lives.

Everyone stood. Cameras flashed and cell phones were raised. Walking toward Cam, Rose envisioned their pasts falling away like the dried-up leaves that swirled in the wind outside. Those painful times were dead and gone. For both of them.

At the altar, her father gave her hand to Cam.

Threading his fingers through hers, of course he winked at her.

In that moment, the future spanned before her and it looked more than bright. It was all new and it was beautiful.

* * * * *

*Pick up the other stories in
Jenna Mindel's* MAPLE SPRINGS *series:*

*FALLING FOR THE MOM-TO-BE
A SOLDIER'S VALENTINE
A TEMPORARY COURTSHIP*

Available now from Love Inspired!

*Find more great reads at
www.LoveInspired.com*

Dear Reader,

Thank you so much for reading the fourth book in my Maple Springs series. I hope you enjoyed the rocky road Cam and Rose took to reach their happily-ever-after. I knew Cam was a troubled soul when he'd lost his biggest sponsor in *A Soldier's Valentine*, but I didn't realize just how deep his shame and distress were until I starting digging into the *whys* that made up his character.

Uncovering Cam's issues with reading came with lots of questions and lots of online research and I only scratched the surface. Dyslexia is a fascinating challenge, one that several well-known folks, including famous authors, have had to overcome. I applaud their grit and determination to master their gifts.

One program that I found amazing in their approach is the Davis Dyslexia Association International at www.dyslexia.com.

All of us have limitations. Some are big and some are small, but all can be covered by trusting in God's grace. Even when life doesn't go the way we think it should, God really can work all things together for good to those who love Him.

I love to hear from readers. Please visit my website at www.jennamindel.com or follow me at www.facebook.com/authorjennamindel or drop me a note c/o Love Inspired Books, 195 Broad-way, 24th floor, New York, NY 10007.

Best wishes,

Jenna